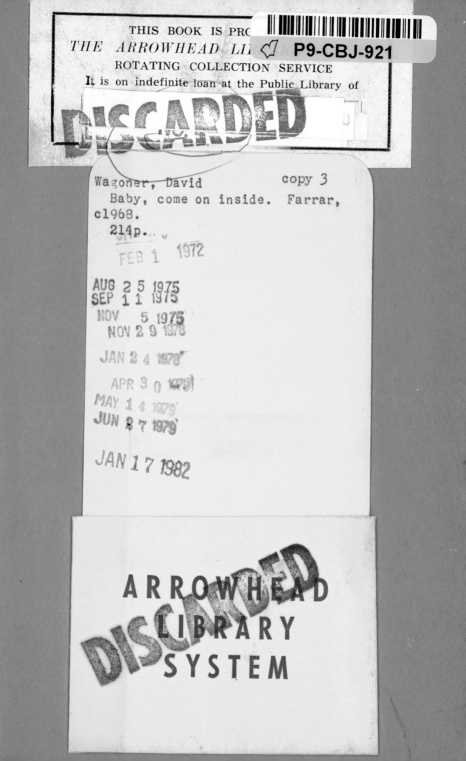

Baby,
Come on Inside

Books by David Wagoner

Novels

The Man in the Middle (1954)
Money Money Money (1955)
Rock (1958)
The Escape Artist (1965)
Baby, Come on Inside (1968)

Poems

Dry Sun, Dry Wind (1953)
A Place to Stand (1958)
The Nesting Ground (1963)
Staying Alive (1966)

DAVID WAGONER

Baby,
Come on Inside

Farrar, Straus and Giroux

New York

for Patt and points south

Baby,
Come on Inside

Take a long stretch, Baby. Are you up or down?
Take your sweet time, Baby. Nobody knows you're
in town.
If you want to see some action, just you stick around.

Chapter one

There wasn't any of that stuff about wondering where he
was when he woke up: Popsy Meadows *knew* he didn't
know. The windows were hotel windows (curtains *and*
drapes), the sheet under his nose was a hotel sheet, and the
phone on the nightstand which practically hit him in the
forehead when he turned was a hotel phone, with ROOM
SERVICE and BELL CAPTAIN and MAIL DESK and so on
around it.

Using both elbows, he levered himself till he was half-
sitting, half-sprawling on the edge of the bed; then he
struggled upright and stood, swaying slightly, in his bare
feet. He kept his eyes off the deep slope of his paunch and
didn't try to taste his mouth yet. At least he wasn't covered
with moss, and there weren't any mushrooms sprouting between his toes. When he saw his red silk robe on a nearby
armchair, he knew he must have gone to bed on purpose.
Or else Sport had been there to help. He wrapped himself

up in it and did a quick tour of the bathroom, shaking hands with three or four handles, splashing his hair out of his eyes (it was getting thinner and curlier in front, but he couldn't check the color because the fluorescent lights made everything dark look like gunmetal) and not singing, not even when he heard the piano going.

It had to be Sport; only Sport used that choppy left hand to cut the sentiment out of ballads. And that meant they were in a suite, which eliminated the possibility he'd torn off on his own some place and wound up in a fleabag. Feeling better, he went to the communicating door, opened it quietly halfway, and leaned against the jamb, cooling his forehead on it.

Sport was playing "Where Am I?" which was either a joke or an accident, and Popsy waited there for a moment, bracing himself, trying to figure out as much on his own as possible so he wouldn't have to ask stupid questions.

It was daylight, so the odds were it was past noon, judging by his normal sleeping habits. But, for instance, which coast were they on? He could see buildings through the haze of the curtains, but they were middle-sized and anonymous. The air-conditioner at the base of one window wasn't turned on full-blast, so that eliminated the southern half of the country: it was late August unless he'd lost track of more than geography. Where had they been going? He tried to think, but his head felt plugged up, as if somebody had stuffed a sock in it. He remembered being in a shower, but had it been outdoors or in the bathroom?

He said, "Okay, Sport, that's enough."

Sport turned on the stool and leaned one elbow on the keys. He managed to reach the floor with both shoes like a man on a tall barstool. "I heard you get up, and I thought you'd like a little music."

"Damn little. I'm hanging over." He took a few steps into the bigger room, which was long and broad and full of low square-edged modern furniture the color of flypaper. "What time is it?"

"Two o'clock our time, four o'clock theirs."

Because he didn't feel too uncertain on his feet, he circled the baby grand and got himself stationed at the window without seeming too obvious about it. Why shouldn't a man look out a window? That's what they were for. He didn't necessarily have to be trying to find out what town he was in. He said, "I'd like some food sent up."

"Which kind of food?"

"Lunch food, dinner food."

"That's what I thought. It's on its way up."

He glanced briefly at Sport's small tight neat razor-burned face, checking his mood, and then looked out the window again. Two hours meant two time zones; so no matter which coast they'd been on, they were in the middle of the damned country somewhere, and most of the middle looked alike, except maybe downtown Chicago. He twitched the curtain aside.

It wasn't downtown Chicago or anything else much either. Brick buildings with flat tarred roofs, nothing higher than a dozen stories or so, a jumble of shops whose signs looked blurred, broad streets, medium traffic, and no trees for three or four blocks in any direction he could see. Palm trees would have been a good clue, but the ones he could make out were elms—or whatever the kind were that looked like magnified broccoli. The lay of the land seemed

5

flat, he couldn't smell any smog, and sometime during the night he must have bitten his tongue: there was a painful lump on the side of it next to his bridge.

Sport said, "Well, how does it look?"

Taking it easy, not giving up yet, Popsy said, "Well, I've seen worse. Water comes out of the faucets, the stoplights go off and on, and they've got streets between the buildings." He took a chance. "What've we got scheduled?"

"How should I know?"

The surprise in Sport's voice was genuine, and Popsy tried to think of something to spread over it quickly. "Would you say I was ahead, behind, or neck-and-neck?"

After a long pause, Sport said, "Well, if you've got to be some place, I'd say maybe you were up against it."

Switching to an easy joshing voice, Popsy said, "Would you say I was too impulsive, Sport?" He got around the piano without bumping it and glanced around for a phone book. "Would you say I'm a creature of whim blown hither and thither by the breeze?"

"You really want me to say *any*thing?"

"Yes: where's a phone book?"

Sport slid off the stool, yanked open a cabinet beside one of the two sofas, took out a phone book, and passed it over without speaking.

He could see it coming: it wasn't thick enough (maybe an inch and a half) to amount to anything, and as he walked off with it, keeping his face away from Sport's sharp eyes, he saw from the cover he was in his hometown. In his hometown, for godsake, what was he doing there? There wasn't enough action in his hometown to keep any-

6

body busy for half an hour, so of course they had to check out right away and find out whether there were even airplanes into this crazy state. But he had to cover up for a little while or Sport would think he was off his head. He said, "How about delivering your learned opinion of the place?" He threw the phone book into a chair, wishing he could tear it in half like the strong-boys in carnivals.

"Inside or outside?"

"The town. Hotels are all alike."

"It's pretty hard to tell, hauling in at night like that." Sport seemed to consider. "I didn't exactly notice much swinging going on, but you can't always tell with these middle-sized places. Look at Kansas City."

"This is no Kansas City. This is the boondocks."

"Lots of things can happen in thirty years."

Popsy jammed his hands into his robe, found a pack of cigarettes, and put one in his mouth without lighting it. "What're you doing, keeping track? How do you know how long it's been?"

"You told me."

There was a knock on the door, and Popsy said, "Well, don't believe everything I tell you."

"I don't." Sport went to answer, his short legs stiff, his blue-and-purple plaid sportcoat glowing in the pale light. He waited with his hand on the knob, looking back at Popsy.

"Answer it, for godsake."

"I'm waiting."

"Oh." Popsy strolled toward the window again with his back to the door and one hand over his face. He heard the door open, the rumble of the room-service cart, and the blah-blah over the check-signing. But he was trying to figure out why he'd come. There must've been a reason. Nobody went down a poisoned well just for the hell of it, and there was nothing here for him but poison. He racked his memory, combed over the recent weeks, and all he came up with were the heavyweight cameras and the mikes and the restaurants and a mish-mash of bad music and scrawling his name. Always scrawling his name on some damned thing or other. And people telling him what percentages were coming out of this or that. If his mother and father had dropped dead of hoof-and-mouth disease, he'd have remembered. It couldn't be a funeral.

He tried to reconstruct where he'd been last: cutting a session in L.A., it seemed like, and nothing had gone right. Was that it? He cleared his throat and tried to imagine holding a note, but couldn't. There didn't seem to be anything inside to push it out.

The door clicked, and Sport said, "It's all yours."

He strolled to the cart and picked up a couple of dish covers and looked at the plastic imitations of meat and vegetables, the salad bowl full of torn-up money some cat had upchucked over. He said, "Where's Freddy? I want a rubdown."

After hesitating, Sport said, "He didn't come along. Don't you remember?"

"Oh, yeah."

"Something the matter, Popsy?"

"No. I just forgot." He didn't feel like telling Sport anything, and he didn't feel like eating. It was a bad combination. For a moment, all he could think of doing was standing still, and that meant more questions.

"You feeling okay?"

"What do you think?" He let his eyes flick over Sport's nosy face again.

"I think you're feeling bad."

He got a piece of toast from the cart, as if he were going to eat it, and said, "Okay, what if you're right? I ask you something, out come the scissors, snip. Quit cutting me up."

"I'm not cutting you up."

"You've been around a long time, Sport. Sometimes you act like an old lady."

Looking hurt, Sport headed for the piano. "I'm not a yes-man."

"You don't bounce any more. You don't like anything." Popsy could feel himself going now, he was getting going, and he didn't want to stop. "Always got your mouth pursed up like a pussycat's dinner whistle."

"A friend's got a right."

"Well, use your left for a while. You're hitting me too often with that other one."

Sport sat down hard on the piano stool and said, "Eat."

"What do you want me to eat for? Do I look skinny?"

"You've got to eat something."

"If you don't like the life, ditch it. You didn't even like that last record." And he hadn't meant to bring that up because he'd have to think about it himself. He tried to think of another subject.

But Sport said, "Did anybody?"

"There you go: snip, snip, the Scissor Man. I need people around me with confidence." He looked at the lousy silk-screened imitation watercolors of Gay Paree bunched around the walls, and tried to remember where confidence

9

came from. *Was* it from other people? Sport started slopping around with some chords on the piano, and he almost shouted at him to shut up, but then he didn't. His eyes went around the room again. "Where's the luggage?"

"Your two suitcases are in your bedroom, mine's across the hall."

"I don't mean that, I mean the luggage." If he could get his notes out, and his journals, and get the right music going, maybe a little extra noise if there was any local talent in women, and get himself organized—get back in charge of things—and have a short drink, he'd be all right. It was a matter of getting the right props, and then his brains would work.

Sport said, "That's all we brought."

"Impossible."

Sport quit playing and stared at him. "You blanked out again."

He sat heavily in the uncomfortable square corner of a sofa and pulled the cart toward him. The dish covers and the starched cone of the napkin were on a level with his chin, and he could see Sport through the water glass, looking like a goldfish. He said, "Well, sort of."

"How far back do you want to be filled in?"

"What's to fill in? We're here. I must've needed a vacation, so why shouldn't I come here? It's my hometown, isn't it? I'm researching my book. You can't expect somebody to remember the names of everything after this many years." He looked around the glass at Sport's face, trying to guess whether he was right. He *felt* right. "I just acted on an impulse, and here we are. If we don't like it, we can go back. I mean if *I* don't like it."

10

"Where were we?" Sport's voice was flat.

"We were in L.A., wise guy, and I got mad in the studio." It was a safe bet, and he could tell he was right by the way Sport didn't jump on him. "So let's just check out and forget it. You shouldn't have let me come without my notes."

Sport came off the stool fast, looking happy and full of energy. "Great, we won't even call her. She won't even know you've been here."

And then he remembered—of course, for godsake, how could he have forgotten?—he was in love with Belle Sanders, and on the third try he jerked himself up out of the deep squat in the pit of the sofa. He turned, but there wasn't any time to swear at it. If they wanted people to sit on the floor, why didn't they just strip the room? He started to take off his robe, then didn't. He had to figure this out.

Sport said, "I'll find out about the planes. It won't take fifteen minutes to get out of here."

He was in love with Belle Sanders, and she was from *here*. That had been the funny part of it: he'd had to chase her here because this was where she came from, a lousy coincidence which had probably been inevitable sooner or later, considering the percentages. He retrieved the phone book and peeled his way through the S's, trying to remember her father's first name.

Still acting happy, Sport said, "Never mind. I'll do it." He took the cradle phone out of the same drawer the book had been in and started to dial.

Popsy yanked the receiver away from him, then had to sit down on the arm of the sofa to collect the phone and the phone book in his lap and untangle the cord from around his elbow. He dialed an outside line and then the number he'd located in half a column of choices. He turned slightly aside from Sport, who was watching him, looking worried, and said, "What's our name?"

Sullenly, Sport said, "Jones."

"That's using the old imagination." He jammed the receiver tighter to his ear as a blurry woman's voice answered, and he said, "I'd like to speak to Belle Sanders, please."

Sport groaned.

The woman said, "She ain't in right now. Back in an hour."

Turning further away till his forehead was almost against the wall, Popsy said, "Who're you?"

The woman sounded annoyed. "What's it to you?"

"Would you please have Miss Sanders call Mr. Jones—" he checked the center of the dial "—Room 905—" he grabbed a book of matches out of the ashtray on the end table and read the cover "—at the Park Tower, as soon as possible."

The woman made him say it again, slower, and then hung up without saying goodbye.

And the trouble was he didn't know whether he'd already figured out a plan of campaign or whether he'd been going to improvise. Sometimes he wrote down things like that among his notes, but he didn't have his notes.

In a resigned voice, Sport said, "What about the plane reservations?"

"Forget it. I'm busy."

"Don't do it, Popsy. It'll be bad for you."

He looked at Sport's small sincere earnest disapproving

12

steady cornball face and said, "What makes you think you know what's going on? Why shouldn't I call her?"

"You want my opinion or you want a yes-man?"

"Get out your knife."

"She's not for you, that's my opinion."

Keeping hold of the phone in case he thought of something or somebody else. Popsy said, "Is that supposed to be unusual? Who *is* for me? The hell with that. *I'm* for *her*."

Sport was shuffling back toward the piano. "I'm just thinking of your own good."

"Well, I'm not, so forget it." He watched Sport get up on his stool like a chimp in an animal act who'd just fouled up a trick. "You can press slacks, and your martinis aren't bad, but you don't know what's going on in my head."

"That's right, I sure don't."

"And speaking of martinis, I'll have one." He saw Sport's face darken. "Or two." He held out the phone and waited, but Sport got up and headed for a cabinet in a corner near the small vestibule. He swung out a pair of doors and began clinking among a cluster of bottles.

Popsy felt impressed. "Is that standard equipment? What kind of a pad is this?"

Looking disgusted, Sport said, "We brought them along."

He tried to remember but couldn't. "Oh, yeah. How? In a sack?"

"Wrapped up in blankets in a suitcase."

"Oh. Was that my idea?"

"Yes."

Feeling nervous, Popsy said, "You know how it is when I get going sometimes. I mean, really get going. I forget. It slips my mind."

"I know." Sport wrestled with an ice tray and, without

looking back, said, "At least this'll finish off Belle for good, and we can get on with something else."

"What's going to finish her off?"

"The publicity. When she gets a good dose of it back in the old hometown."

He could feel the anger clearing his head. "What publicity, you little nut? Nobody knows I'm here. I don't know who *you* are, but I'm Jones in 905."

"Are you kidding?" Sport started dropping cubes in a tall mixer. "Richie's coming. And Tess. And Mary-Mary. And probably Alice, no matter what she said. And Warbucks."

"What?" He couldn't believe it. The phone book slid out of his lap and scraped his bare ankle on the way to the floor, and he held onto the phone in case he needed something to throw.

Sport said, "And everybody else too, probably. That's what happens, isn't it? I'm surprised half of them aren't here already."

"For godsake, who spilled it?"

Sport gave him a puzzled look. "How's it going to stay quiet? With them around, every reporter in this hick state's going to come banging on the door."

"What did you do to me?"

"Me?"

"Sport, you must've *known* I didn't want everybody rattling along after me like a bunch of tin cans. How am I—?" How was he going to keep track of Belle if somebody was throwing a party at him? It was bad enough trying to handle her sober.

"You don't remember?"

14

"Remember what?" He tried to sort out what he had to do, and he started pacing with the phone, giving it a shake now and then till the bell tinkled inside it. "This is worse than scissors. They're getting out the cleavers. That did it, Sport. You're canned. I never thought you'd—"

"*You* called them."

"Very funny. Work it up as a routine. I'll give you a three-minute bit in my next benefit." He dropped the phone into a chair and headed for the bedroom, untying his robe as he went. It was suddenly important to get dressed in case he had to cut out in a hurry.

Sport raised his voice, going boy-soprano. "You spent half an hour on the phone last night after we got in."

It was darker in the bedroom—the drapes were pulled almost shut—and the smell of dead booze mixed with disinfectant (or whatever the hotel used between guests) made him shake his head as if somebody had cracked an ammonia ampoule under his nose, and he raised his voice too, though it was bad for the throat. "You're cuckoo! You expect me to believe that? You must've left your marbles in your other head." He gave himself a dim smile in the dresser mirror as he went by, jutting his chin to pull the slight bag up under his jawline.

Sport was behind him in the doorway, stirring the pitcher. "Okay, when they come piling in, just ask them."

He turned on the bright bathroom light and the fan and the overhead heater, and took the gray elastic gut-belt from the towel shelf, where it lay in a neat row with a pair of shorts, socks, and a handkerchief. He said, "It's impossible."

"I didn't think you were really bad. You didn't seem bad." Sport was in the bathroom doorway now.

Turning his back, he struggled into the belt with his robe on, pulling the springy elastic up till it was hauling in most of the slump below his waist. "Impossible." But he knew he was only saying it to keep himself feeling okay for another minute.

"You honestly don't remember?"

He held up the striped boxer shorts in front of him like a tabloid. They looked too big till he tried them on. "No." Then he peeled off the robe and threw it into the shower behind him. He said, "Sport, are you putting me on?"

Holding up his free hand, Sport said, "My mother."

Popsy took a long look at himself in the mirror, and it wasn't much fun. His face looked as big as a pie plate, and though the excess weight hadn't begun to make him squint over his cheeks yet, his eyes seemed smaller than before: less of the whites showed. And his mouth looked very big. "My big mouth. How did I seem? I mean, I didn't sing or anything like that, did I?"

"No. You were just geared up."

"I'm warning you, Sport. If this is a gag, you can hang up your jock. I'd be very very mean." He caught Sport's eye at an angle in the mirror and interrupted him before he could start. "Ever had a big old stage-mother—who thinks you just wrecked her kid's career for good—ever have one tell you what she'd like to do to you? At the top of her voice? For ten minutes?"

"No."

"Then imagine it. That's what I'd do to you. I won't waste the energy describing it."

Sport made a gesture, almost spilling the pitcher. "Now I'll tell *you* something."

"You have to admit I wasn't boozed. I know how I'd feel today, it's like a gauge."

Sport said, "No, you weren't really loaded. But if you don't know what you're doing, you'd better not do anything. If you get sued again, Kitch is gonna have a fit."

Popsy felt his stomach wanting to sink, but the belt caught it. "Did I call him?"

"Not while I was listening. But how long do you think it'll take him to hear? He can hear a dollar bill falling before it hits the floor."

He gave himself another long look, then plugged in his electric razor and started on the black-and-white stubble. "At least I had enough sense not to call Kitch. I used to walk in my sleep. Maybe I—" He remembered the tangle of arguments and cross-talk and garble—or some of it— from the past week or more. It was as if somebody had cracked the days and dropped them all in a mixer. "There's been too much pressure, too much pushing. The minute I turn around, somebody plants his hands on me and pushes."

When Sport started to fade back into the dim bedroom, Popsy grabbed a water glass off the rack and held it out. "Don't go away with that." He kept on shaving till he felt the glass turn cold against his fingers.

Sport said, "Take it easy," and left the doorway again.

As he dressed (his slacks were wrinkled in the seat, his pale-blue sportcoat had a coffee stain on one cuff, the only clean shirt he could find had had its collar crushed), he felt warmer, and maybe it wasn't such a bad idea having a few people around as long as he didn't let things get out of control. He yanked the drapes open to help locate his shoes (one looked like it had been stepped on by a first-baseman) and had another look at his hometown while he was at it.

Nobody was getting raped or held up on any of the roofs he could see, and nothing was on fire. There were no tornadoes on the horizon, and no earthquake fissures were gobbling up the parked cars on what he now recognized as Main Street below him. It was all there, apparently behaving itself, waiting for him to make something of it. He found a spare necktie rolled up like a confetti streamer in his suitcase and put it on, and when he found himself starting to think about his mother and his old man, he shouted, "Hey, Sport!" And when the small head appeared in the connecting doorway, he said, "Get on the stick. I want two pairs of slacks, charcoal and gray. Three shirts, pink, yellow, and what-the-hell. See if I brought any socks. Two pairs of loafers, tan and black. See if the hi-fi in the other room works and check the needle and get a dozen records, no singing." He maneuvered the necktie knot into position. "Not even me. I want to think about something else for a change."

"You do?"

Sport sounded genuinely surprised, and it made him mad. "Yes! And get some cans of peanuts and the local paper and the address of a good sauna that doesn't have a bunch of fags hanging from the pipes. And if anybody calls, I'm Jones. Does the manager know?"

Sport said, "Don't you remember? The night clerk didn't even see you come in. I was talking to him, and—"

"No, I don't remember! How should I know what we did? What did you do, make me walk up nine flights of stairs? Maybe that's why I'm—"

"Automatic elevator!" Sport was raising his voice too.

18

Popsy waved him away. "Get moving. If all the knives and scissors and hatchets and bolos and cleavers and razors around here started going at once, there wouldn't be anything but hamburger for miles around. I know the way you guys think."

"What guys?"

"Guys like you. You work for somebody for years, and then you want to either cut in or cut out."

"Don't get all worked up, Popsy."

"Don't tell me what to do. I'm telling *you:* go shopping before the stores close. Only ninety-five shopping days left till Christmas." He looked out the window again, through the streaked dust on the glass. No hills, no rivers, damn few trees, no natural obstacles, and he felt like a general surveying tough terrain. House-to-house fighting, maybe. Building-to-building. Somebody was going to get hurt, as usual.

His voice fading through the other room toward the door, Sport said, "Happy birthday, boss." The door slammed.

And Popsy thought it over, feeling depressed. There wasn't anything for him to count. August was right, and the memory came sneaking into both ears and up his nose and into his mouth. If it wasn't yesterday, it was today, and if it wasn't today, it was tomorrow. So it was all the same thing. He was running over a birthday, a bad one, the worst kind—with a zero on the end of it. He was turning fifty, and why had he come back here to this place to make it even worse?

*Remember me, Baby? I'm the one that didn't when
you did.
Remember me, Baby? I was the pot and you were
the lid.
I've known you forwards and backwards from a
goat to a kid.*

Chapter two

He hurried down the corridor toward the elevators, and
things weren't so bad after all. The shave and a couple of
drinks had put a new complexion on things, and on him
too, and all he had to do was sneak out before Sport got
back, use the side entrance or the alley or whatever they
had, catch a cab to No Man's Land, and make like the
Caliph of Baghdad spending a night in disguise among the
peasants. He'd have to pick up a hat some place and something to use as a mustache maybe.

The carpet was new in the hall, and the walls had been
painted recently, and maybe the town was pulling itself together. It hadn't had a hotel that didn't stink back in his
day. He remembered, after he'd started cutting records,
the clamor and all the screwy offers he'd had from locals
to come back and emcee the Corncob Festival and the State
Eagles' Convention Ball and other outstanding events—and
the pleasure he'd taken thinking up new ways to say no.

He punched the button and did a little soft-shoe for his own benefit in the narrow panel of mirror between elevators. He couldn't see both sides of his body at once: don't diet, buy a skinny mirror.

But when he heard the elevator coming, he started backing up, and after listening hard to make sure, he was running back along the corridor toward the suite. There was no mistaking the sound: ordinary people didn't holler in elevators, not that many *different* people. He could smell reporters and photographers, and he made it back to the right door and had himself inside looking through a slit before they all spilled out, like a stream of clowns coming out of a midget car in a circus, and started down the corridor toward him with Richie, that damned Richie and a girl, leading the way, his straight black oily hair and his sun-lamped face gleaming.

Popsy shut the door and leaned against it, trying to think, but he hadn't had any ideas before Richie was pounding on it—it had to be him doing bossa-nova rimshots and double paradiddles—and there was no conceivable way to get him to quit. If Richie wanted to get through a door, he got through it, even if it meant using a fire ax or buying the doorman for his own nightclub, and Popsy opened it six inches, bracing his whole weight against the heavy panels. Without showing his face around the edge, he said, "Get in here, Richie!"

One arm, one shoulder, and one leg came through in a wrinkled tuxedo, but Richie was still facing outward saying, "Love and kisses!" A flashgun went off, then another. "That's it. Love and kisses!"

Popsy pulled hard at the arm, and the big head came

through the slit for a moment, said, "Whoa, boy," and went out again.

Other people were talking, trying to get him to pose for this and that, asking questions, but Richie said, "Sliced peaches! Save some film for the big brush-fire. Sliced peaches!" The flashguns went off again. "Abercrombie and Fitch!"

Getting a fresh grip, Popsy pulled him all the way into the room and slammed the door.

Richie said, "Hey, take it easy on the dry goods. And don't forget my baggage." He handed Popsy a half-full highball glass, then opened the door to a slit again and reached out without looking. "Have to find the right handle. Ah!" He pulled the girl inside, scraping her against the jamb as the flashguns popped.

Chaining the door, Popsy walked away from them, rubbing his forehead. It was going to be one of those evenings.

Richie said, "The least you could've done is pick some town on a direct flight, Popsy."

"The name is Jones."

"That plane landed and took off so often, the stewardess never *did* get her blouse buttoned."

Popsy leaned against the bar cabinet, trying to sort himself out. He looked at the girl, who was dressed in a very short shiny pink sheath and who looked more like a piece of candy than anything else. She had silver hair that swooped under her jaw on both sides. "Is this her?"

Richie said, "Naw, this is Miss Armory."

Looking awestruck, the girl said, "Emery, Sally Emery. I'm very happy to meet you, Mr. Meadows."

Though he felt halfhearted about it, Popsy said, "Jones."

"Jones." She seemed flustered. "It's an honor. I have all your records."

"I wondered where they'd disappeared to." Because Richie laughed at that, Popsy felt a little better. "What was all the fireworks in the hall?"

Retrieving his drink, Richie toasted them both and sipped it. "They followed me in from the airport. Nice guys. That's one thing you can say in favor of the sticks: at least you don't have to buy space in the papers. It's a pleasure to do business with hungry reporters."

Popsy shook his head wearily. "Honest to God, Richie, sometimes— If I wanted pictures, would I call myself Jones?"

"They weren't taking you, they were taking me."

"And me," Miss Emery said.

"Wouldn't you say you might've aroused a little curiosity?" Popsy aimed his thumb at the door. "Wouldn't you say they might possibly be still out there? Like for a week maybe? Camping?"

Richie glanced around. "Who you got in here, the First Lady?"

"No."

"Well, what kind of a party *is* this? For shut-ins? Agoraphobes Anonymous?"

Miss Emery said, "I know what that means."

Pulling open the bar cabinet, Popsy said, "Oh, the hell with it. Have a drink." He watched Richie finish his highball and come for more, and he got out of the way and wandered past the piano, trying to think. He didn't feel up or down, and he didn't know whether he wanted to be in or out.

Miss Emery said, "It means you're afraid of wide-open spaces."

"So don't open yours too wide, there, Miss Armory." Richie opened a bottle of bourbon.

She said, "When Richie told me we were coming to see you, I couldn't believe it. It was like having a dream come true."

"That so?" The natural light was fading out of the streets, and Popsy watched it go, wanting it to leave faster. The mixture of neon and mercury vapor light meant action, even the little there was here. He needed some action.

Richie said, "Miss Armory's a model—"

"I thought maybe she was."

"—who wants to be an actress—"

Miss Emery said, "Emery."

"Believe it or not," Popsy said.

"—but she just hasn't had any kind of lucky break which is what you need in the rough game of showbiz if you're going to get to the top—"

"You have to have talent too," Miss Emery said.

"—and see your name up in lights and climb that stairway to the stars."

Popsy said, "And you have to've had your heart broken like an old toy balloon."

She looked serious. "Oh, I hope not."

"And you have to climb into millions of little boxes in millions of little homes across this unsanforized country of ours and let your face hang out so far and so lovably it wants to fall off," Popsy said.

In a low voice Miss Emery said, "He means TV."

Richie said, "Oh."

24

Miss Emery said, "Do you think I'd have a chance on TV, Mr. Meadows?"

He examined her, giving her his doctor look. "Miss, you'd even have a chance on the Dodgers."

"You could be the Game of the Week."

She said, "I don't like being kidded."

The door opened the length of its chain, and Sport got enough of his face through to be recognizable. Beyond him, people were asking a thick muddle of questions, and a flash-gun went off. Popsy hurried to the door, shut it far enough to slip the chain, then braced himself against it while Sport squeezed through with a double armload of packages. Somebody else's arm and foot started to come through too, but he stomped on the foot and clamped the door briefly on the wrist, and both pulled back. He shut the door again and chained it.

Sport said, "They aren't sure you're here yet, but it won't be long." He dumped one of the packages on top of the hi-fi, nodded disgustedly at Richie, and headed for the bedroom with the rest.

"How's old Winter Sport?" Richie said, but there wasn't any answer.

Still at the door, feeling the hum and buzz of conversation behind him in the corridor, Popsy said, "Don't you ever go anywhere quietly, Rich? Those guys'll never leave now."

"What's wrong with publicity all of a sudden?" Coming over close, Richie said, "Stop me if I'm wrong, but I don't detect any party going on in your head." His tanned, deeply creased handsome beat-up-looking face was only a foot away.

Popsy joined the inspection, and they went over each other's features like makeup men looking for trouble. Richie seemed to have plenty of his own: his eyes were bloodshot, and even though the bags under them were firm-looking (how did he exercise *them* for godsake?), they were there all right, and you had to put in a lot of night work to earn that size. Back when they'd both been just plain stand-up comedians looking for a good place to sit down, they hadn't been very friendly: if their agents weren't feuding, then some club-owner would be trying to bid them down against each other. But TV had loosened things up, and Popsy had started singing and recording, and Richie could just barely carry a tune, and now they could put their arms around each other's shoulders, on camera or off, without checking for knife holes later. You could even call them friends, and they'd both done it from time to time.

Richie said, "Last night you sounded good for a week."

"You heard me, huh?"

"Heard you? What do you mean, heard you?"

"Nothing." Popsy saw Sport come edging nervously into the room again, and he tried to ignore him. "Nothing, moods change."

"All right, so it's called on account of rain. I'll fold up my girl and go."

"Stick around. I'll snap out of it."

"This is your hometown, isn't it? You got home-folks trouble?"

He could tell Richie was trying to be helpful, but he knew his own eyes were turning shifty. "No, let's have a drink."

"Is it a dame?"

Popsy shrugged himself away from the wall and looked

around for something to do. He took the short stack of records out of the paper bag and shuffled through them.

Richie said, "It's a dame." He snapped his fingers four or five times, looking at Sport. "It's that what's-her-name. The one he had at the beach."

Sport turned aside and put the phone book away, and Popsy took a big-band album out of the stack and slit the plastic cover with his thumbnail. But he couldn't get it on the turntable fast enough: there was too much noise and too much silence in the damned room.

Richie said, "Don't let her get you down."

"Well, I'm down."

"Get up, man, get up. She's not worth it."

"The hell she isn't."

Miss Emery said, "What's her name?"

Richie looked at her sitting on the edge of a sofa cushion, then shrugged apologetically at Popsy, who said, "It's okay, don't worry."

Raising her voice a little, Miss Emery said, "I mean, sometimes advice from a stranger can be very useful, so pardon *me*." Her skirt was halfway up her thighs, and she was keeping her plump suntanned knees together.

Richie said gently, "Listen, little muffin, little puffy muffin with the butter running down the sides, made out of whole bran, are you going to be good for our digestion or not?"

"A man has to chase a woman slow." She looked stubborn.

"Out of the mouths of babes. You hear that, Popsy?"

Something inside him was squirming, trying to get out because it didn't have enough room. He put an unlit cigarette in his mouth, but getting air through the filter made him feel as if his face was collapsing. He said, "If you don't mind, I'm going to keep my private life where it belongs."

Richie said, "Like in *Life* magazine."

"Like in my pants." For instance, Richie hadn't even remembered it was his birthday, and how was that for friendship?

Looking at Sport, Richie said, "What's the verdict? No game today?"

"I think it's been called," Sport said.

"Says who?" Popsy could feel himself getting hot in the face. "Let's not get scissor-happy around here."

"Scissors?" Richie looked puzzled.

"Specialty of the house. Everybody's doing it: manicure scissors, upholstery shears, hair trimmers—"

Miss Emery said, "My mother can make gardenias out of marshmallows." She noticed Richie's blank look. "With scissors. For parties. You know." She twiddled her fingers.

Richie said, "She just leaves them laying around?"

"Decorating salads and things." She waited during the brief silence, then said, "It was just a remark."

As if pulling himself together, Richie said, "Well, it's too bad. We could've worked this up into something. Trying a new town's always fun for a while: everybody gets their pictures in the paper, the cops all have reasonable prices for a couple of days at least. I mean, there isn't a middle-sized city in the country that isn't okay for a couple of laughs. But if nobody's going to play—"

Popsy lifted the tone arm onto the slowly spinning record, and the brass came blaring out of the multiple speakers. Raising his voice, he said, "Stick around. Nobody's pooping out."

28

Miss Emery said, "*I've* got an idea." She got up and headed for Popsy, holding out one hand, and when he crossed his forearm in front of him defensively, she took it as if he were an escort. "Mr. Meadows, I'd love to hear you sing. How about an oldie like 'Just One of Those Things' or 'Lover'? Play for him, Sport. We can listen to records any old time, but— Come on, now, be a sport." She laughed.

Not moving when she tugged him, Popsy said, "I've got a frog in my throat. A big one."

"Miss Armory, lay off," Richie said.

"He just wants to be coaxed a little." She tugged again.

Looking at Popsy seriously, Richie said, "You got a cold? Better watch yourself. You sounded kind of funny on the phone."

"Nothing's wrong. I said I had a frog in my throat, not a doorknob." He leaned down at the girl till his nose almost touched hers. "I don't feel like singing, Miss Emery. *You* sing."

"I asked you first. Don't try to wiggle out of it."

He said, "Sing anything. I don't care if it's a Serbian folk song."

"Singing isn't exactly my long suit."

"What is?"

Richie said, "Diamonds."

"I mean, I sing in the shower, but—"

Popsy said, "Take a shower then."

"But I don't have a trained voice like yours."

"It's very easy," Popsy said. "First you have to train it to go on a newspaper, and then you—"

Richie said, "*I'll* sing."

29

"Let's all sing," Miss Emery said.

Disengaging his arm, Popsy left the joke behind, and Richie said, "Anybody else coming? Or am I your one and only?"

Wearily Popsy said, "Everybody's coming."

"Not that bunch of bags too?"

Like a man making an announcement, Sport raised his voice over the record. "They're here already. I dodged them in the lobby."

Richie said, "Holy smoke, Ladies' Day. You must be scared of that dame, Popsy, or you wouldn't want so much help. I mean interference."

"I'm not scared of any dame," Popsy said.

"Don't be crazy, man, don't say that. A couple of old buddies of mine named Samson and John the Baptist said that to me once, and they haven't been around lately."

"Quit giving me advice. What am I, a beginner? If I want to feel this way or that way, I'll feel it."

Miss Emery said, "I guess nobody wants to sing."

Richie shooed her and took Popsy's arm himself. "We're just vocalizing a little here first, Armory, that's how the pros do it." He walked Popsy toward the windows. "All right, better get married and get over it."

"That's the general idea."

" 'Better to marry than to burn.' "

"Who said anything about burning?" But he did feel terribly hot in the face and wondered whether it showed. He wasn't sweating, just hot, and he spat the unlit cigarette onto the carpet. "I've been married lots of times, and it never seemed to help the temperature very much. I've been frozen and warmed over and cooled off and burnt." He

30

looked Richie full in the face and lowered his voice. "What's going on? What do you think?"

"If you have to ask, that's bad." Richie seemed uneasy.

Somebody started beating on the door, and Popsy signaled Sport to take care of it and, at the same time, wished there were other signals that would work like "Get Me Out of Here" and "Cut, We're Running Overtime" and "Come Back Tomorrow, We'll Try It Again." But he could only wave one hand vaguely, which he didn't like the looks of: it was the color of a fish's belly, too long, too narrow, and he'd been forgetting to bite his fingernails. They were long too.

And then the door was slapping backwards against the wall, and from the far side of the room he could see fat Mary-Mary wearing some kind of sequined monstrosity and behind her Theresa looking like Clark Gable with her hair cut short and behind her Alice the Foaming Cleanser in some kind of white evening dress torn raggedly at the knees, maybe on purpose, and they all came parading into the room with Mary-Mary carrying a cake like a stack of newspapers on which five candles burned. Sport was trying to direct traffic, trying to get the door squeezed half-shut again, but the two slick-looking young guys following the women got past him; and beyond them Popsy saw the cameras with flashguns attached going up in the air over all the heads, aiming into the room toward him.

He ducked and got one hand over the lower part of his face, and then Mary-Mary was coming at him, leaning backwards away from the candle smoke which was going up under her chin. They were all talking at once, and Richie was helping Sport make a loud commotion at the door, which he finally heard shut. Nobody thought to turn down the hi-fi, and it was okay with him: the less he understood from here on, the better he'd like it. He was getting a great big closeup of Mary-Mary's bridgework as she opened and closed her mouth. He glanced away and saw Theresa and Alice were doing the same thing, and as he eased himself back into the tenor's corner of the baby grand, it dawned on him they were singing Happy Birthday. Mary-Mary had powdered her whole chest, and sweat was wearing a darker waterway down into the cleavage. Theresa and Alice were both trying to smile as they sang, and his mind was beginning to feel wiped out to the last man.

They finished and kissed him, and he held still for it, watching the lipstick come swooping up at him and feeling it smear the edges of his mouth with three near-misses. Then they introduced the young guys, who each gave him a hearty sincere handshake almost as good as an assistant producer's, and Richie started talking and pouring drinks, and Sport started cracking ice, and Mary-Mary got the cake centrally located on the flat piano top.

Theresa said, "Is this where we sign up for the Peace Corps?"

It took Richie a few moments to shout everybody down, which meant he'd thought of a good one and wanted everyone to hear it, then he said, "Tessie, if they ever sent you to an underdeveloped country, you'd—you'd—" (he was revising it in his head, Popsy could tell) "—you'd double their gross national product overnight. If you aren't the grossest national product I've ever seen, I—" But the others started razzing and talking as soon as he'd made the point.

Then Miss Emery was up close, looking dazzled and thrilled and giddy, and she jiggled Popsy's elbow and stage-whispered, "It's just like the 'Tonight Show.'" She gave him some more lipstick on the side of his face.

Alice said, "Blow out the candles before they burn out. It's bad luck."

To Mary-Mary, Miss Emery said, "I've always been one of your greatest admirers."

"Me too," Mary-Mary said. "Who're you?"

Feeling a strange kind of halfhearted energy manipulating his jaw, Popsy said, "That's a newcomer to the wonderful world of showbiz, the up-and-coming choir leader Miss Armory, who's about to corner the sing-along market with her good-natured joshing and her open-throated golden alto voice."

Swirling a highball, Theresa said, "What's up?" Her purple silk Chinese-looking suit had a high collar and calf-length pants. "Do we get convention badges? Or are we on our own?"

"We're all here waiting around the rabbit hole to see what's going to come out," Richie said.

Popsy said, "What am I, the hole or the rabbit?" He felt annoyed.

Alice imitated a slinky walk, but her bony elbows and knees and pelvis stuck out like weapons. She leaned back against him. "Which do you want to be, Popsy? We could take turns."

He shifted away from her, and the big band kept blasting away, making his head shake by itself. He took a deep breath, and as long as he had one inside him—and nothing in particular to do with it—he bent over the piano and blew out the four candles that were still lit, watching the wax spill onto the frosting and harden there like tiny pink eggs. He looked out the window, where the sky had darkened to a luminous violet. There was such a weird difference between the inside and the outside of himself. Like the inside and outside of a hotel.

The general talk started again, and people seemed to be leaving him alone; but then Mary-Mary was at his elbow, speaking in her normal gravelly voice. She said, "I deduce you're in a slump, Popsy. Your face is on crooked, your ears don't match, your neck isn't quite filling up your collar, you aren't chain-smoking, you haven't been on the telephone for at least three minutes, Sport looks mad, and as long as you're picking a phony name, why not Schwepperman or Angostura? Jones means you weren't out for laughs. It's a bad sign."

He gave her a good look. "Are you a friend of mine?"

"Yes."

"Then lay off. I'm holding myself together here as a favor to everybody. If I ever let go, there's going to be some wreckage."

"Something bad?"

"Right. In B-flat."

Mary-Mary hawked but didn't spit. "What's the matter, you trying to please the younger generation?"

"Think I'm nuts?"

"You don't have any kids, do you? Some I don't know about?" She leaned beside him, trying to inspect his face.

"No."

"Then it's a woman again. Don't you ever get tired?"

"Yes. Like now."

"Tell you what you do," Mary-Mary said. "Get your

mind off it. Think up some new material for me, my show opens in five weeks. I need some new sight gags."

Coming up behind her, Richie said, "Never mind, if the sight of you doesn't make them gag, you'll never get off the ground."

And so, as the sun sank slowly in the west for a change, instead of the northeast, he left the beautiful shores of Mary-Mary and Richie with reluctant heart and watched Alice and Sport start playing four-handed piano against what the record was doing. And he had enough of that in five seconds and had to turn away and try to catch anybody's eye.

One of the young guys came up to him. "Mr. Meadows, that last one of yours was the smoothest, grooviest platter I ever heard. Absolute silk. I don't know who was arranging for you—"

"Mort Haberman," Popsy said sullenly, automatically.

"—but it was really a high kick. How many sessions did it take?"

"I forget." Popsy started toward Sport, who was rummaging in the bar cabinet.

But the young guy held his arm and said, "I understand it isn't doing too well, not as well as it should, if you ask me. And I think maybe I know why."

Popsy held still for it. "Why?"

"It's a little complicated. Maybe I could see you alone sometime and show you on tape and paper. Out loud and in black and white. I have a lot of clients with fresh ideas."

Glancing over the young guy's full head of hair, the glossy complexion, and the whole set of very very narrow clothes he was wearing, Popsy felt like keeping his mouth shut. He let one side of it sag, nodded slightly, and went straight for Sport, managing not to talk to Theresa or Miss Emery, who had their shoes off and were matching foot sizes. He hauled Sport out of the noise into the bedroom and half closed the door behind them.

Sport said, "Don't blame me."

"Shut up a minute." Somehow he felt he didn't have much time. "Instructions. Rent the next two connecting rooms, whichever way they go. If you can't get two, get one next to yours." He took the roll out of his pants pocket and peeled off a hundred. "Tell the manager I want the hall cleaned out, and if that means hiring a cop or two—it probably does—then do it. Tell him we'll keep the party going with room service, that'll make him happy. This phone's going to start ringing like a bastard as soon as the word gets out who all's here, so get to the switchboard. I want it kept clear except for long distance. *I* have to give the okay about who comes in, personally. I don't want Alice or somebody rounding up the whole floor or Tessie falling for the cleaning lady. If I'm not here, you're in charge." He peeled off another hundred and some twenties. "Spread it around a little, but a C-note for the manager and half that for the night man."

Sport said, "Sure."

"And don't look at me like that. It's my birthday, isn't it? And we're here in the great big fat murmuring heart-land of America, and it's summer, and the moths are all out screwing each other in midair. What more do you want?"

"Nothing."

He examined Sport's tight tough face. Like a walnut. "Now before you get going, I want you to pass me a nice medium highball without letting a lot of flies in here. I'm going to be out of it for a while. Business." He ignored the suspicious look. "Move it."

Through a slit in the door he watched Sport cross to the bar and mix him a drink, but before he could start back with it, there was another commotion at the outside door. Sport talked for a moment past the taut chain, then slipped it and let in squat, broad-shouldered Chris Michelson, who was already hollering at the top of his voice the way he liked to do, and right after him, hanging on like a drunk trying to catch up with a lamppost, Warren Buxton, good old Warbucks, with his hairpiece dangling inside out half over his forehead. Popsy braced the door and took a deep breath. He must have called everybody after all, and this was apparently going to be a pretty good party, if you liked that sort of thing.

He shut and bolted the door, turned on the bedstand light so he could read his pocket address book, and dialed direct to Julie's apartment in New York. Settling back on the unmade bed, he waited for her voice, and it came— sharp, precise, as if she'd been interrupted: "Hello?"

He said, "Hi, sweetie."

"Who's this?"

"Don't kid me." He turned off the light without knocking it over and took a good look at the darkness. "It's me."

"Well, if it isn't the golden voice of the jukebox. I didn't recognize you in monaural."

"No overdubbing, no nothing. Just little old me." He didn't like the sound of her. Too much edge. "How's your hammer hanging?"

"Popsy, you don't ask a woman that. You ask a man."

"Some people have them and some people don't."

She turned brisk suddenly like a saleslady. "Look, I'm putting a little dinner together here for some friends, and I—"

"Okay, forget it, some other time." He listened hard, testing, and her answer came so fast he knew she was all right.

She said, "Well, did I win six easy lessons or something? Is this a giveaway program?"

"No."

"You answering requests from your many many fans?"

"No."

"Too bad. I have a wonderful request for you."

He raised his voice as somebody turned up the hi-fi in the next room. "Don't tell me. I'm calling for a very specific, very down-to-earth reason. I want you to come see me."

"Are you dead?"

"Come on."

"Because that's when I'll come and see you."

But some of the hardness had gone out of her voice, and he kept his own soft now and kind of sad, even if he could hardly hear himself. "What've you got to be bitter about?"

She said, "Stick out your tongue. If it stays out and turns black, let me know."

Now somebody was knocking on the connecting door, and he pulled up the bedcover and ducked under it with the receiver. He said, "How are things in your end of the swamp?"

"Pretty good, so don't rock the boat." She paused for a second. "It sounds like a party."

"That's neighbors. I'm alone."

"You aren't calling me 'chick,' Popsy, and you aren't

saying 'cool it' or telling me you just 'blew your mind.'
What happened to that kind of talk?"

"I'm just talking. Do you have to analyze it?"

"How's the book?"

"At the moment it's just like me: lousy. L-O-U-E-I-A-
W-S-I-E-Y. Lousy. Thanks to you."

"Me?" She sounded genuinely surprised. "Don't blame
me. You haven't called for months. Besides, I must've given
you some good dialogue over the years."

"You should see it when it's written down."

She said, "If you're including any of those nightclub
routines you used to do, no wonder you feel bad."

The knocking stopped, and he lowered the cover to let
some air in. "Always running me down."

"Every chance I get," she said crisply. "Careful crossing
the street."

He let his voice go deep and simple. "Something's wrong,
Julie."

"With you?"

"Yes."

"Go on, tell me. Make me happy."

Trying to keep it casual, he said, "Something's breaking
up inside me. The doc says there's nothing there, but—"

"Maybe it's that glass heart. It wouldn't show up on an
X-ray."

He put his legs over the side of the bed and sat up.
"Don't be a bitch. Would I call you if I didn't need help?
Would I take all this backchat?"

"I'll admit it's unusual."

"I haven't sworn at you once."

"Once."

He tried to remember. "Well, once. Is that normal?"

39

"Nothing you do is normal. Who're you crucifying nowadays?"

He turned on the nightstand light so he could see himself, but there wasn't any mirror nearby. "Leave Jesus out of it. Never mind feeling sorry for Jesus. Feel sorry for me."

"I don't have anything to feel sorry with. You busted my sorry machine."

"Now listen." He struggled up and carried the phone to the dresser top so he could keep track of himself in the mirror. He looked like somebody who'd just spent a night in a haunted house. "I want some honest advice from someone who knows me."

Her voice went flat and slow. "I know you."

"And don't say you know me too well." He tried to push some energy into her over the long wire. "If you've had your fun, I'd like to ask you a serious question."

"You'd better turn up the bass a little, boy, I'm getting some wow on the tweeter."

"Seriously." He paused. "Do you think I should get married again? Do you think I can make it?"

"With who?"

He fished around for an answer, and the most disturbing one he could think of was the truth. "Well, she's kind of young."

"How young?"

"Pretty young."

"Twelve? Thirteen?"

"Early twenties."

There was a long pause. Then she said, "How should I know? How's your blood pressure?"

40

"I'm not talking about physically. *I'll* worry about that."

"You should."

He gestured at himself with one hand like a salesman making a pitch. "I mean mentally. Psychologically."

"Who knows? You never slow down enough to hear yourself think. And why don't you ask your latest ex instead of me? Her memory's probably fresher. Unless she's insane, which wouldn't surprise me."

"The hell with her." He leaned close to check the whites of his eyes in the mirror, and they had cracks in them like old plaster. "I want *you* to come. I *want* to hear myself think for a change. I need somebody like you who knows me and doesn't give a damn about me. And you're the toughest one I know."

She sounded flattered. "Ah, hell, Popsy."

"You *are*. You could save my life."

"Why should I want to save your life?"

But she sounded tired now, and it was a good sign. He said, "I'll leave you alone. I won't so much as lift a paw."

"Ah, hell."

"Come on, be a good enemy."

"Can't we do it over the phone? I've got company coming. Go on, spill it if you want to talk."

Without pushing too hard, he said, "I need to see you, sweetie. You know I'm no good over the phone. I close up."

"Ah, hell."

"I'm only in Philadelphia. At the Bellevue Plaza. Eighth floor, name of Parsons. It'd only take you an hour."

"I'll lose a whole day at the shop."

She was weakening fast, and he tried to sound very practical. "I'll get you back on a plane. Or better yet, let somebody else milk those rich bags for a day. Don't you want to watch me suffer? It'll add years to your life."

"Okay, okay. I'm a sucker."

"No, you're not." Because her voice sounded so limp, he tried to spruce her up a little bit, to keep her from trying to call back right away. "You're an angel. Eighth floor, Parsons, no funny business."

"Okay." She hung up.

He waited in front of the mirror, thumping himself on the side of the head with the receiver in time to some rock number that was on the hi-fi now; but then he had to quit because he'd started doing it too hard. Sending her to Philadelphia would keep her busy for a while, though you could never tell with Julie; she was pretty smart sometimes and might dope it out before she even left Manhattan. Why had he felt like doing it? He put the receiver back where it belonged and headed for the bathroom.

By the ghastly fluorescent light he inspected his face, trying to figure out some way to disguise it—at least temporarily, till he could get out of the hotel. He could cut off some hair and paste it under his nose, or there was enough gauze on the roll in his toilet kit to reach around his head four or five times à la the Invisible Man. Better yet, he fished out a box of different-sized Band-Aids and began peeling off the plastic backing. He put a large regular strip across his upper lip like a pink mustache and a round one the size of a half dollar on his right cheekbone. He covered the middle of his forehead down to his eyebrows with a square as big as a soda cracker and put another regular strip along the left side of his jaw.

42

He wasn't sure what he looked like, but he didn't look much like Popsy Meadows, which was just fine with him; and if he had to wrap and seal himself like his own birthday present, that was fine too. He got his slate-gray narrow-brimmed summer straw out of the closet where someone, maybe himself, had put it last night, and pulled it down snug over half the forehead bandage. Sport had hung up the new clothes, but he didn't want to take time to change now. He checked the mirror again, liking the crumpled shirt and the stained pale-blue sportcoat; they made him look like a real hometowner.

He opened his mouth to sing a line of Happy Birthday, crinkling the bandage on his lip, and when nothing came out except a couple of phlegmy crackles from deep in his throat, he remembered *that* about yesterday too, he remembered how his voice had fallen out of his voice box—good old Larynx and Pharynx, the Singing Twins—and had landed in his stomach and been digested right on the spot, and he got out of the bathroom before the memory made him sick.

Slipping the chain on his own outside door, he opened it an inch and inspected the local talent: two photographers and a guy who looked like a reporter, three high-school girls in miniskirts—probably after Richie—and a woman who might be anything, a stringer for a news magazine maybe. They were between him and the elevators, so he'd have to go the other way; and before he could hesitate and get the twitters, he had shut the door silently behind him and was walking swiftly toward a red STAIRWAY sign at the end of the corridor.

A man said, "Hey!" behind him, and then "Hey, you!"

But he kept going, listening hard, and as soon as he heard the feet coming, he broke into a run and got through the opaque door and up the bare cement stairs to the tenth floor before anyone had decided whether to chase him seriously. He ran on the thick carpet all the way to the elevators, skidded without stopping, and headed off at a right angle down the corridor of the other wing to a second STAIRWAY sign, passing an open-mouthed old woman who covered her chest with her purse as he went by. Once on the stairs, he took his time going down, catching his breath one gulp at a time. It didn't taste very good, and whether it was going in or out, he couldn't detect any trace of music in it.

Get moving, Baby. Don't do anything too long.
Give us the runaround, Baby, and you can't go
wrong.
If anybody keeps up with you and me, bring 'em
along.

Chapter three

It was what seemed to be a new place called The Coop,
the closest thing to a nightclub he could find in a hurry,
and he was past the hatcheck girl with his hat still on and
into the gloom and smog of the main room before he took
it off. When the sleek-looking short maître d' came toward
him, Popsy slid sideways along the bar where it was darker
and got up on the last stool behind a square pillar where he
could see more than half the stage and have a good excuse
for keeping his back toward the bartender.

He ordered Jack Daniel's without turning around and
then watched the fat Sophie Tucker-type, wearing enough
makeup to scrape up a fresco of herself with, go blimping
around the stage with a hand mike. She was being backed
by a flimsy, old-fashioned trio—who probably swept out
the place regularly and did Polish weddings on Sundays—
a bass, sax, and accordian, and she was singing:

> *There's so little of you*
> *And so much of me,*
> *You're getting a great big bargain:*
> *Half of me would be free.*
> *If you couldn't finish me all*
> *Before you went to sleep,*
> *You could wrap me up in your arms:*
> *The rest of me would keep.*

And so on. He jiggled his knee to keep time and sipped his drink, feeling the whiskey soak the bandage on his lip. Even when he tried to sop at it with a paper napkin, the fumes kept going up his nose. And he couldn't figure out what the atmosphere had to do with anything: he'd spent years in places like this, backstage, out front, eating, table-hopping, signing tabs, trying to hit the one note that would make people shut up and hold onto their silverware and feel moved or at least impressed, even though most of them probably didn't have enough equipment in their heads or hearts to feel anything besides themselves. How many times had he died onstage before he'd found out what those right notes were?—the ones that could even get through the numbskulls and the half-crocked, mattress-backed little hookers that made up half the mob in joints everywhere, the hard haunting rough-edged notes that came out of the throat of the animal living inside him.

The woman was singing:

> *I may look like the end of a Greyhound Bus,*
> *But anyway nothing's bigger than both of us.*
> *I'm the giant family size . . .*

A B-girl came switching up to him, arch and demure, wearing something long in red mesh, looking as though

46

she'd been caught in a fishnet and had given up after struggling halfway out of it. She said, "Hi, there."

He nodded and got a good grip on his hat and his drink in case he had to take off in a hurry.

She said, "Have an accident?"

There was an old answer to that (No thanks, I just had one) but he didn't say it. He touched each of the bandages with the thumb of his drinking hand; they were all in place.

She said, "Don't I know you?"

"I work out at the packing plant."

"Oh, that's nice." She shrugged one shoulder and touched his knee. "How about buying me a drink?"

She wasn't bad-looking, and he remembered the hundreds and hundreds and hundreds of them, in droves and clumps and clusters, maybe learning to shuffle through a couple of dance steps in the dead early afternoons, lavishing all their concentration on lighting and dragging at cigarettes, the taut or jiggly behinds, their breasts at attention, uplifted as much as possible. What happened to them all? Did they ever become housewives, or did they just keep getting in and out of bed with guys like him, who didn't dare tell them apart, till nobody asked for them any more?

He said, "You're a nice girl. Go away."

"Smart ass."

She was ready to sting now, alert and angry, and he checked her over from top to bottom. Being mad would make her feel better for half an hour, and he was glad to help her out, but one more word from him would overdo it. He smiled instead, feeling the bandage stretch, and she walked away.

And what was he getting sentimental about? The spit

47

and cigarette butts on the floor, the mixture of sweat, booze, and perfume in the air, and all the faces around him —fresh ones, some not so fresh, beginning to slide down past their own cheekbones, and some already sagging into thick puddles around the jowls—who'd come in to pay for a little noise or to trade insults or get drunk or try hustling somebody. For them it was always the best kind of night in a nightclub: a night with walls around it so nothing really dangerous could fly in, a night with a level floor under it (even if you couldn't see it, you knew it was level —unless you happened to fall downstairs), not like the night outdoors full of cracks in sidewalks and alleys and open manholes and bushes and gullies and men in black masks and animals slobbering out of luminous mouths. In here you could pretend you'd just said something funny or would have said it if it wasn't so noisy, or could pretend you were waiting for somebody to come back or show up any minute (it was like being on duty, you could feel like a sentry in a nightclub), or you could brood—there was no better place to grow grievances; it was like a greenhouse, like a black-and-white house. Or if you weren't alone, you could sit with somebody without being with her, could be in a play for your own benefit: a lot of people *saw* you looking like a couple, so you *were* a couple, maybe even a newspaper item, and it halfway made you feel like a couple.

Some punk kid was on the stage now, yammering into the mike with his own introduction that didn't leave any room for the audience to laugh or groan—which they wouldn't have done anyway, since they were talking as loud as the kid—and he was thin and geared up and sweating through a white turtleneck. A set of traps and an electric guitar quieted everybody down a little, and the kid started into a song, his voice as scrawny and sharp as he was. At first it was slow and easy:

> I know a way to get a girl.
> Just listen, buddy, and I'll fill you in.
> You don't need talent or the will to win.
> Write her this letter, and you'll see.
> Take it from me.

Then the drums and guitar went into a heavy rock-beat, and the kid held the mike a quarter inch from his lower lip.

> Dear So-and-so,
> You've got to let me go . . .

and the rest disappeared into the jangle and blare.

Popsy scooped up his change, unsnarled the rest of the coins from his pants pocket, and headed for the phone booth around a corner near the johns. He knew how to get a girl too, and not by writing any damned letter (when had he last written anybody a letter?) or by howling and jerking. He slid into the booth, checked his address book, gave the number, shoved in the coins, then opened the door just enough to make the light go off.

On the third ring Stutz answered, and before he could get a whole sentence out, she said, "My God, Popsy, don't tell me you're in town. I was just going out."

"Are you cuckoo? What would I be doing in Miami?"

"I don't know." She paused. "What do you usually do anywhere?"

"Okay, come on."

"Come on where? What?"

He kept his voice matter-of-fact, straightforward. "Come on where I am. Let's kick it around again for a while."

"You mean now?"

"Sure."

"Shack up, you mean?"

"I mean let's give it another try."

There was a long pause, during which she started a couple of words, then swallowed them. Then she said, "What's the matter with you? You crazy? I'm only ten years younger than you."

"You look great."

"That practically makes me an old lady."

He let himself sound fairly enthusiastic. "You look great."

"How would *you* know? You haven't seen me since—"

"You look great."

She hesitated again. "Don't start cutting the cake before you even light the candles."

"See? You remembered my birthday." He was oddly pleased, and it worried him. Was he running that short of admiration? He said, "It's turning out bad. I could sure use you."

"What's the matter, didn't anybody come over to play with you?"

"Don't sound bitter, honey. It's out of character."

Her voice went up a couple of notes. "You haven't had a good word for me for—how long? You had thousands of chances to at least say hello."

"Hello. " He shifted on the narrow seat and tried bracing his knee against the metal wall, but the angle was wrong. The kid on stage was still chewing the mike.

"That time on Broadway, right out in front of the theater, you stuck your tongue out at me."

"I was just trying to remind you of something. Give me a break. What have you got to lose?"

"You sound pretty sober."

"Cold."

"I can lose my goddamn mind, that's what I can lose."

A couple of girls in their early twenties minced past the booth, their tight skirts riding high, and he opened the slit a little further to watch them go into the ladies' room. He said, "All the magazine articles about husbands say I'm at a dangerous age."

"I believe it. I think you've got a screw loose, Popsy."

"Then come on back and screw it tight for me." She was making him mad, and he tested his mind by listening to the kid singing: his voice was shifting from white throaty to thick throaty as he kept half swallowing and coughing up his own tongue. And the kid was going to wind up with nothing in his mouth or his throat, just a clean empty hole like an air-shaft, out of which nothing could come but bad air.

She was saying, "This is just a momentary whatsit. Lapse. You had a little collapse on your birthday, and you want Mama to kiss it and make it well."

"Don't needle me. I'm making you an offer."

"That sounds very romantic, like an option conference."

He knew his voice wasn't helping him any, and he tried to focus it. "You were always magic for me, Stutz. You can still be a bearcat if you want to. I know you. You're still turning over inside, hard and fast."

"Leave my insides out of this. You don't know my insides any more."

"I know them."

51

"The hell you do. I've even had some of them out."

He looked at the receiver. "Which ones?"

"Never mind which ones."

"Anything important?"

"Nothing *you'd* notice."

The girls came out of the ladies' room, or were they different ones? He didn't remember the faces, but the behinds seemed the same. Something inside his head didn't want to concentrate. He said, "Well, if it's gone, you can't lose it again, so don't worry."

"I've got plenty more to lose, believe me. You're a specialist at guts, and you'd have all mine out in a week. I can't do it, Popsy, I'm too shaky nowadays. I was just going out to a movie."

The operator interrupted, and he had to feed the kitty again before he could say, "I'm talking about Palm Springs, not a movie."

"You don't know *what* you're talking about."

He said, "Or Baja. Or Tangier. Name it and we'll dig it."

"I'm married again."

"So what?" He couldn't remember whether he'd known that or not.

"How come you want me? I mean, you can have your pick, can't you? You always could. They haven't stopped crumpling up around you, have they?"

"I just step over them, Stutz."

"Why me?"

"I've got a feeling like unfinished business."

"Romance!" Her tone was bitter again.

"All right, I use funny language. I can't help it. I'm talking out of my emotions, not my brains. I need you, I'm desperate. I'm going to twist the damn phone in half trying to keep from bawling." He gave the receiver a little twist and thought about bawling. He'd have to try it again sometime because he couldn't remember what he looked like when he was doing it.

She said, "Popsy."

"It's weird."

"It's weird all right." She paused. "I never heard you talk like—"

"So will you come on and meet me?"

"My husband—"

"Take your husband and stick him."

"My husband's away on business, so I—"

"Get here."

She said, "Where?"

"I'm in Chicago at the Hilton. Name of Edwards, Room 810."

"All right, I've got it. Chicago isn't Palm Springs."

"Meet me here, and we'll go together."

"All right." Her voice went deeper and deader. "I'm getting sick already. I can feel it."

"Come on, we'll get sick together."

"Okay, Popsy. Anybody going to say *love?*"

"Later maybe. I've got a case of champagne in the shower. I'll go turn on the cold water."

"Okay, just don't get in there yourself."

The operator interrupted again, and Popsy gave her a couple of quarters, and then everybody hung up. And the trouble was, as soon as you hung up, you were hung up. He opened the booth door and stuck his feet out into the hallway, but the voice of the kid singer started up again, and there was no way to get comfortable. How many minutes were they giving somebody that raw?

53

Going back to the bar, intending to stay there just long enough to think of somebody else to call, he wedged himself backwards onto the only empty stool and ordered a drink over his shoulder.

"Take your hat off," the bartender said.

He took it off without arguing, and that was a good sign. He nodded, congratulating himself. And no matter how much it hurt, he concentrated on the singer, trying to figure out what made the kid's voice so unpleasant.

He was wearing skin-tight tan slacks, pelvis forward with the mike cord trailing between his legs, and his white turtleneck glared in the spotlight; and he was still trying to milk applause from his last number (instead of covering up the gaps with whatever his line of chatter was), even though most of the customers had their hands full of drinks and each other and the only clapping was coming from his mother, his wife, and his agent—or whoever was trying to whoop it up for him at ringside. And Popsy felt very sorry for all the things the kid had to learn yet, if he was going to last long enough onstage to learn anything, which was doubtful.

But it wasn't much better when he started to talk: he bragged about how popular his next number had been at the last place he'd sung, and all the time his eyes were shooting around the room, looking for any kind of good reaction or good news, and explaining to everybody what a "novelty number" was.

Popsy finished his highball in one slug and handed it back, jarring the man next to him with his elbow, and the electric guitar went thumping into the beat with the drums, and the kid sang:

I broke the record
For the most times left behind.
I broke the record
For the fastest change of mind . . .

and he started breaking old 78's over his knee and his head and letting the pieces scatter around the stage.

Nudging the man next to him, Popsy said, "He isn't resonating pharyngeally."

The man leaned backwards a little and said, "What?"

"He's trying to do it with his mouth." Popsy shook his head sadly and glanced at the man. "You can't do it with your mouth."

"You're goddamn right I can't."

The bartender said something, and Popsy said, "You've got to do it with your throat."

The kid sang:

I broke the record
For the most times up the pole.
I broke the record
For the most times in the hole . . .

The bartender tapped Popsy on the shoulder and said, "Simmer down, buddy, and watch the nice floor show."

"What do you think I'm doing?"

"I don't know." The bartender had the fresh drink, but he wasn't handing it over. "What do *you* think you're doing?"

"I'm giving the kid a singing lesson. He needs it."

The man on the next stool said, "Try to come in for a quiet drink."

"Tell you what you do." The bartender turned Popsy

on his stool till his knees were shoving against the man. "You turn around and have your last drink, and then you give him his lesson later when he's not so busy."

The man shoved at Popsy's knees angrily. "Get away from me."

Righting himself, Popsy twisted and reached backward for his drink, taking it before the bartender could change his mind. He said, "I know what I'm talking about. If you try to do it with your mouth instead of your throat, you start getting your jaw locked almost shut like the kid's is, and then the tone goes for the nose, and you've had it."

"I'm going to give you a little voice lesson in a minute," the bartender said. "I told you to keep it down."

"It *is* down. If I ever let it go, it'd break your mirror."

The man on the next stool finished his drink hurriedly, got off, and backed away to watch.

"You're going to break what?" the bartender said.

Popsy got off his stool too and went to lean in the shadow of the pillar near the end of the bar. The kid was finishing his record-breaking number, and the small stage was strewn with chunks of Bakelite, some still held together by the record labels. The applause was scattered again, and he listened to it critically, recognizing the exact instant when the kid should have cut it short and covered it up. But it went on almost five seconds too long, dwindling and separating into individual claps.

Then the bartender was hauling backwards on Popsy's arm. He said, "No standing."

"I'm not in anybody's way." Popsy shook his arm free, crooking his drinking arm and balancing his glass against his coat lapel.

"You're going to need a lot more bandages if you act like this, bud."

Popsy fished out a five-dollar bill without spilling anything and gave it to the bartender. And the kid was making another mistake (now he was introducing a new number) by littering up his own stage. If he had to break records at all, it should have been as a finish so somebody else would be stuck with the mess. As it was, he'd have to crunch around on his own garbage for at least another five minutes. And furthermore, some of the pieces had spilled over the edge of the four-foot-high stage (some of the people at ringside were looking at them and passing them around), and you should never give anybody in an audience anything they could throw back at you.

The bartender said, "You know, you look an awful lot like Popsy Meadows."

"My cousin." And especially nothing as lethal as a jagged chunk of record which could come skimming back and put your eye out.

The electric guitar started booming again, its amplifier shaking against the red backdrop where the two accompanists had been jammed out of the range of the spotlight, and the kid sang:

> *When I was a baby, man,*
> *I used a BB gun.*
> *It went ping ping*
> *And didn't hurt no one.*
> *Gonna get my gun again someday, baby,*
> *Gonna get my gun again.*

Now somebody else was pulling at his arm, but he had to concentrate because the kid's tone was awful and someone ought to tell him, someone ought to do something about it before he wrecked his vocal chords and made his name bad on the circuit.

The kid sang:

> *When I was twenty-two,*
> *I used a .22.*
> *It went pow pow*
> *But I missed you.*
> *Gonna get my gun again someday, baby,*
> *Gonna get my gun again.*

A waiter in a tux, carrying a big menu, was joggling him and staring up sideways at him.

The bartender said, "See what I mean?"

"Jesus Christ," the waiter said. "It *is* Popsy." He hesitated. "Isn't it?"

Popsy jammed his hat on and had some of his drink, and unfortunately, no matter how good he happened to feel, how sure of his opinion he was at the moment, he was going to have to get out of here before it turned into Gang Busters.

Clinging hard to his arm now, the waiter said, "Get Mike!" to the bartender like a sergeant, then shifted voice to honey-sweet toward Popsy: "What happened to your face, Mr. Meadows? Anything we can do for you?" He leaned around the pillar and shouted "Ringside!" at somebody.

Wobbling a little at the noise, the kid sang:

> *When I was thirty-eight,*
> *I used a .38.*
> *It went bang bang*
> *But I was too late.*

> *Gonna get my gun again someday, baby,*
> *Gonna get my gun again.*

And what the hell was the idea of singing inappropriate material? The kid wasn't even near twenty-eight, let alone thirty-eight, and it was as bad as having some beautiful babe sing a love song meant for a male voice. The kid must have an idiot for a manager, or else he was his own idiot.

The waiter said, "Right this way, Mr. Meadows. How're you feeling?" He tried to haul Popsy forward.

But he hung back and said, "You must be out of your mind. My name's Billy Jangles." He didn't want to get into any ringside crunch of autographing and table-skipping. Not now.

The kid sang:

> *When I was forty-four.*
> *I used a .44.*
> *It went boom boom*
> *But you slammed the door.*
> *Gonna get my gun again someday, baby,*
> *Gonna get my gun again.*

But what looked like the maître d' and somebody in a business suit were weaving fast between tables, looking desperately happy, and he had to think of something quick. One good thing about the kid anyway: he didn't stop for a hassle, at least not a simple hassle—nobody had started throwing broken records at him yet.

The drummer did a hop, skip, and a whack, and the kid sang:

> *Now I'm pushing fifty*
> *And it's fifty-fifty*

Between me and her.
Maybe I'm just the wrong caliber.
Maybe she don't want me
Dead or alive . . .

The maître d' jammed the waiter out of the way, grinned, held onto Popsy's coat sleeve and said, "Mr. Meadows, I'd like you to meet the owner who I'm sure is overwhelmed to have you with us tonight and would be glad to pick up any reasonable tab if you wouldn't mind taking a bow so the folks can get a load of you. Mr. Felber, this is Popsy Meadows, who as you know—"

The song was finished, and during the uncertain applause—which he would have joined if he could have trusted anybody to hold his drink and if the owner hadn't been trying to shake his other hand—Popsy saw the kid heading offstage, and he aimed himself at the curtained arch labeled EXIT because even if it didn't lead to the dressing rooms, it would at least get him out into the alley.

The owner said, "This is an enormous thrill because I—"

Popsy couldn't shake the maître d' loose from his sleeve, but he managed to bring him along through the red plush curtains and into the relative quiet of a short L-shaped corridor running parallel with the back of the stage.

"If there's anything we can do for you—" the maître d' said, his voice strained, high, and terribly friendly. He made an okay-get-out-of-the-way gesture with the menu at a bouncer-type lounging in the bend of the corridor.

Popsy said, "I want to talk to that kid singer."

"Yes," the maître d' said. "Yes, of course, Sergio Cantare." Then over his shoulder, "He wants to talk to Sergio."

Looking back, Popsy saw the owner, the waiter, the bar-

60

tender, the man who'd been on the stool next to him, a couple of B-girls, and other miscellaneous heads bobbing forward through the arch. The red curtains were hanging straight in, as if being blown by a wind.

The maître d' said, "I happen to own a piece of him I'm happy to say he has a great future wasn't he wonderful?"

The kid was standing in a doorway at the other end of the corridor, his mouth open, looking uncertain whether to run, hide, take a bow, or what. And the maître d' managed to get ahead of the pack, grinning and jabbering in both directions and waving his menu as if there'd be no problem about getting a good table right away in the corridor.

Getting a firm hold on Popsy's shoulder, the owner shouted above it, then had to reach over it to get hold of the maître d' by the ear and shout again, "A photographer, you dumb sonofabitch. Get on the phone."

Popsy tried to say something to the kid, who was looking at him with a kind of awed hesitation, not believing it yet, but there was too much noise.

The man who'd been on the next stool said, "I didn't know it was you, see?"

Using both elbows and stiffening his legs, the maître d' was trying to keep from getting pushed right past the doorway and along the hallway. He finally hooked one arm around the jamb and started talking to the kid.

Somebody whisked off Popsy's hat from behind. He made a grab for it, missed, then concentrated on getting through the doorway without breaking any ribs. The owner came right behind him, like the other half of a horse, and as the kid backed out of the way, the owner and the maître d' got the door half closed with most of the maître d' on

61

the outside. Each started a furious simultaneous monologue, and then the owner straight-armed him in the face, got him all the way out saying, "Photographer, photographer, photographer, photographer!" and shouldered the door shut and bolted it. He turned around breathing heavily, sweating, and smiling, and he opened his mouth to go on talking.

Popsy said, "Shut up." He took a look at the room, which was one of those dressing rooms, all right: the walls weren't actually sweating, but they had been, and the mirrors at the littered dressing tables were peeling as if somebody had been shaving the silver off the backside with a razor.

The kid looked awed. "Mr. Meadows? What's the matter with your face?"

"Never mind." Popsy touched his Band-Aids to make sure none were flapping loose, and bringing up the subject of faces wasn't the best idea because the kid had on enough Ruddy Juvenile #6 to get him onto a reservation. Popsy studied his broken-looking nose, his deep-set eyes, his oily black curls. He said, "Kid, what's your name again?"

"Sergio Cantare."

The owner said, "Sergio Cantare. It's Italian."

Some kind of rumpus had started outside the door, but that was the way doors were: usually there was a quiet side and a loud side, and it didn't matter which side you were on, the quiets wanted it quieter and the louds wanted it louder. Popsy said, "Well, Serge, I have to tell you you've got a sloppy act."

"That's right," the owner said. "The best in the business."

62

The kid seemed grateful for the news. "You really think so, Mr. Meadows?"

"Your timing's lousy, your arrangements are lousy, your material's lousy, your tone's worse than lousy, and you aren't thinking at all out there. Not at all. Zero."

"You want to buy a piece of him?" the owner said. Someone started rapping on the door, and the owner turned around angrily and started rapping back on the same spot.

"But you've got possibilities," Popsy said.

The corners of the kid's wide mouth turned up slightly. "I can dance too."

Popsy said, "Let me give you a little advice."

"Jesus, I'd be so grateful for anything you want to tell me, Mr. Meadows. You're famous for your advice. I read that article in *Esquire* where you were shaping up some young singer because she didn't ever look at anybody— any one person, I mean—in the audience for longer than a second, and you said—"

"Do you mind?" Popsy said.

"I'm a little nervous." The kid wiped his hands quickly on a stained towel. "I've never seen you with bandages on, I guess."

The owner said, "Now if any money's going to change hands, I think we ought to get Sergio's agent here. Not that I trust the bastard, but at least he knows how to keep from getting axed completely."

"Will you just stay out of this, Mr. Felber?" the kid said.

"What?" The owner's brow went crinkling all the way up into his thin widow's peak. "Who the hell do you think you are?"

Popsy said, "Shut up."

The owner smiled grimly and nodded, his eyes watery with the effort.

"Maybe I better just drop you a line sometime, kid." He checked the single window—frosted glass with chicken wire embedded in it—and it was low enough and wide enough. He shoved a chair under it, knocked the heavy latch and swung it up. When he stood on the chair, the dirty ledge hit him in the thighs.

The owner said, "My God, you can't go yet!"

"Now wait," the kid said. "How'm I going to know what to do?"

He got one leg outside, straddling the ledge and ducking his head under the sloping glass. "It'd take too long, kid. I don't want to start anything I can't finish, and that creep's going to have half the city in here before long." He let himself down into the alley without spraining or tearing anything.

And the kid came right out after him, bouncing down onto the cinders in his pointed patent-leather pumps.

The owner's head and shoulders came out the window. "You can't do this to me, think of the publicity, I mean where's the percentage?"

Popsy started down the alley toward the lighted sidewalk, feeling uncertain, and when he glanced at the kid's eager, excited, happy, electrified, brainless look—the kind that meant "I'm really where it's happening"—he felt a little sick to his stomach. Something was in there, not food of course, but something, and it couldn't stay there, it had to make a move. Which meant he needed a drink.

You're a big man, Baby, 'specially round these parts.
They teach you in night school like the Crafts and
Arts.
If you've had enough fits, Baby, now you can have
some starts.

Chapter four

As they made a left turn into a different alley three blocks
away, the kid was saying, "I'm not really Italian, I'm part
Greek and part Jew like a hot meatball, but it's better for
the box office."

He'd been going on and on like that, and Popsy blinked
to clear his head. "What box office? Since when do they
have box offices at clubs?"

"You don't think I'm gonna stick in the small time, do
you? I've got plans," and he went on talking.

But Popsy was smelling the alley and the exhaust from
cars and the faint gluey smell from the packing plant,
which had to work hard to compete from way out at the
edge of town, and the frying meat being exhausted out of
the rear end of an all-night café, and the dead steam puffing
through somebody's wool slacks at the cleaner's, and the
suddenly wild, sweet odor which meant rotten fruit behind
a grocery—his hometown was getting into his sinuses if

nowhere else—and when the kid led him toward a solid metal door propped open with a two-by-four, they passed the richest combination of all somewhere at the foot of the dark bricks, as pungent and acrid as the aftermath of an explosion, a distillation of the others, urine and puke.

The kid said, "I mean, how the hell could I get any bookings with a name like Morris Locotos?" He slipped through the door without stopping.

Popsy tripped slightly over the raised doorstep, then followed past the GENTLEMEN and LADIES into a dark smoke-crammed joint about a third the size of the last one. The stage was just an enlargement of the middle of the bar where a rose-colored spotlight shone on the deserted traps and microphone. The kid ducked to the right and slid along the leather seat of a corner booth, and Popsy followed. It had to be a dump that was very sure of itself or else it had young waiters in track shoes, because leaving an easy back door open, a gangway for deadbeats, seemed like odd business. But he was grateful he didn't have to come parading in the front like an emcee starting an old-fashioned conga line. He put one hand over most of his face, checking the bandages, till their drinks arrived. The bandages felt good, and maybe he'd just leave them on till they fell off.

The kid was saying, "You've always been my ideal. I always knew I'd meet you some day because I've been patterning myself on you."

Half the bourbon went home where it belonged, like a letter with a big check in it, and Popsy said, "Then you're going at it ass-backwards, kid. I spent ten years as a comic."

"Yeah, but I'm not funny."

"What difference does that make?" He could feel his eyes starting to slide around in search of a telephone, and he deliberately dragged them back and aimed them at the ice in his glass. "You don't have to be funny to be a comic. Tell jokes instead. Go listen to what other guys are saying in other clubs on your night off or between shows. Then come back and do whatever you can remember. Whatever you steal without writing it down is your style. That's how you find out what your style is. Nothing to it. Except ulcers."

The kid looked as if he were soaking it up like a bar rag. "You think I ought to put some comedy in, huh? Between songs? You know any writers who aren't working?"

"Kid, you've got a stage presence like somebody making an announcement at the junior prom."

"Little too formal, huh?" The kid was hunched forward over his crossed forearms. "Jesus, I can't believe I'm really talking to you. You."

"Where's the folk songs? Why aren't you screaming with some acid-rock bunch? What's the matter with you? You're an anachronism."

"What's that?"

"You're studying to be a has-been. I expected you to start crooning out there any minute. That guitar's just a cover up." But he didn't feel as interested as he had been. Something in his mind was going away from the booth; it was getting up and walking purposefully out the front door and signaling a cab and going back to the hotel to see whether the party was rare, medium, or well done. Under the table his feet felt light and swollen inside his shoes, like balloons.

The kid said, "What do you do all day? What do you think about?"

Taking a good look at the kid's expression to make sure it wasn't a put-on, Popsy kept his own face out of the way for the few moments it took the waitress to give them fresh drinks, then said, "I float on a big plastic sea horse full of self-esteem, kid. I decide which of my twenty-five agents and managers is going to be the human sacrifice of the afternoon, and I sing a little for him. No matter what he says, I can him. Then I call up two or three dames and knock a couple of them down, saving one for the middle of the night—like raiding the icebox, you know?—and in-between times I work on a book, rehash arrangements, straighten out all my confused friends, spend lots of money, or try to keep the top of my head from blowing off and hurting somebody, and if there's any time left over, I drink. As soon as I figure I've drunk too much, I eat too much." The kid was listening like a portable tape recorder, and Popsy kept his voice below the level of the general hubbub in the place. "It makes for a full day, especially if you've got any doctor's appointments, rehearsals, sick animals, weddings, interviews—weddings are a lot of trouble because you have to break so many engagements first—court appearances, parades, previews, and once in a while, believe it or not, I have to go to the john."

"Yeah?"

"I know it doesn't sound possible, but I can prove it." He was coasting now, didn't have to push, could just coast, and it would last for hours unless he really ran into something hard. He started to slide out of the leather seat and head for the john.

But the kid said, "I want to make the big time. I'm tired of singing in these little peanut machines in hick towns." He leaned sideways, earnest, frowning, breathing through his mouth. "How about a break? Help me get booked into New York."

"Too soon." Popsy struggled upright, feeling the booze trickle down into his feet and lower his point of gravity till he was like one of those round-bottomed clowns you couldn't knock over.

"Or L.A. Or any place."

"You need seasoning, kid. You haven't been cooked yet. You've got lots of raw meat but no gravy." He went around the corner into the hallway, then turned left under GENTLEMEN and got himself into a vacant stall, and it was a little bit like being a horse: if somebody had thrown a blanket over him, he could have fallen asleep on his feet— or a nosebag and he could have eaten himself into a stupor. But there was only the urinal with a cake of moth-killer in it in case too many moths came flying out of people's pants, and one other customer in a plaid sportcoat who was having a nice long refreshing look at himself in the mirror while he combed his straight gray hair.

When Popsy focused his eyes sharply, he caught the other staring at him and tried to look neutral or preoccupied, but it never worked. It was always the same process when a man started to recognize him: at first, whoever it was would go dead calm, then begin getting mad for no reason. He'd tried to figure it out over the years, and it had to be some kind of envy—or else some emotion he didn't know anything about. A guy who might turn out to be very friendly later on always got mad first.

69

He tried to speed it up, but he couldn't go fast enough, and the man said, "Looks like you really caught a couple."

"That's right." Level voice, faintly pleasant, no offense —Popsy tried it but knew it wouldn't do any good.

The man said, "Not being nosy, but don't I know you from some place?" He shifted his broad shoulders so he could look at Popsy straight.

"Not a chance."

"Well, you don't have to be a pain in the ass about it." The man was scowling now. "Ordinary friendly question."

Using a slightly higher voice so he wouldn't sound like himself, Popsy said, "I'm just minding my own business."

"What kind of a fruity wisecrack is that supposed to be?"

A little angry now, over the edge of the stall he said, "Look, man, you're shutting off my water. Leave me alone." But that wasn't going to work either because the man was having another look at himself in the mirror, thinking up what to say next. Popsy zipped and started out.

The man said, "Now wait a minute. You want to step out in the alley and wise off like that?"

But Popsy let the john door swing shut behind him and ducked back into the booth. The kid wasn't there, but he spotted him jawing with a good-looking girl farther down the bar at the foot of the small stage. And the trouble with tying one on was that he always seemed to get the ropes tangled around a bunch of irrelevant people in the process. There were more drinks on the table, so he helped himself to the one that smelled best. And the other trouble was he knew he didn't have a chance of getting himself to call Belle tonight because by now he didn't know what he'd say to her: marry me, carry me, or beat it. And if his voice

70

was really soluble in alcohol, why hadn't it dissolved years ago? Why had it waited till now? He'd always imagined coughing it up eventually, like some kind of gristly knot, half chewed but still squawking by itself, on a bad morning in his late sixties maybe—it would look like some kind of wireless transistorized bug, and it would turn out somebody else had been doing the singing all these years and had planted the gimmick in his throat and had been broadcasting through Radio Station Popsy Meadows from some crib in the back of a skid-road bar. But just to have it suddenly melt and slide down his throat like a chunk of sherbet—

And the other trouble was the man in the plaid sportcoat from the john was leaning over the table, looking dark-red in the face and saying, "Just what's the idea, buddy?"

It was too gloomy and smoky in the bar to read the man's expression accurately, but Popsy got ready to duck. He didn't quite get ready fast enough. Taking almost no backswing, the man hit him a glancing blow right on the cheekbone bandage, and after a certain amount of commotion—during which he let himself down sideways on the leather seat and a couple of highball glasses came bouncing and spilling past him to crash on the floor—the kid was back, scuffling and arguing.

The man said something, and the kid said, "You jerk, that's Popsy Meadows!" and Popsy sat halfway up in time to see the kid get him medium-hard on the nose. Two bartenders were coming; and holding his nose with one hand, the kid said, "Popsy Meadows!"

The man said, "Who?" And then the bartenders had his arms wrenched up behind him and his feet almost off the floor.

71

Scooping up some of the ice on the table, the kid sat down quickly, cupped it in both hands, and stuck his nose in. He said something, but it was too muffled.

Popsy got a twenty out of his pocket as fast as he could and handed it to one of the bartenders, saying, "Just keep him away from here." It had happened so fast, only the people at the next two booths and a few at the bar had stood up or turned around to look.

The man said, "Hey, it really is." His wrenched arms were forcing him to bow over the table, but he smiled. "Say, it's a real pleasure, Mr. Meadows."

With the bartender who'd taken the twenty leading the way, they hoisted him straight out the back.

Finding a drink that hadn't spilled, Popsy held it against the base of the kid's skull, remembering the rudiments of nightclub first-aid.

But the kid jerked away from it and took his nose out of his hands. "It won't bleed. It never bleeds. It just gets swollen shut inside, damn it. What time is it?"

"I don't know." He'd quit wearing a watch years before. If people wanted him to be some place at a certain time, that was their problem.

"I have to do another show at eleven, and I'll sound like a kazoo."

A combo started rattling away on the little stage—amplified flute, bass, and drums—and the lights went up there and down everywhere else. The numbness was wearing off his cheekbone; it had begun to throb under the Band-Aid, and although it didn't seem too likely, it was possible a shiner could spread from there to his eye.

One of the bartenders—the one who hadn't gotten any

money—was standing a few feet away, peering close, hesitating. He was skinny and middle-aged, and when he came closer, he said, "Is that really you, Mr. Meadows?"

"We need a bowl of ice and a couple of clean hand towels."

"I used to watch you play football," the bartender said. "You were a senior when I was a freshman." He smiled, and his uppers were false.

Popsy gave him a twenty. "I'm not here. Keep it quiet, will you?"

"Sure, sure."

"Ice."

The bartender went away, and the kid said, "That damn nose of mine, I ought to have it clipped."

Several customers were still standing around uncertainly at the edge of the next booth, trying to get a good look through the bad light, and Popsy put his hand over half his face and said, "Quit thinking about your nose. That's most of your trouble. Instead of having a nose job, get your mind off it. Okay, the nasal pharynx is part of anybody's resonance, but it's *back* of the nose, and when you get out there crouched around the mike like a robot with his first erection, your chest muscles and your shoulders and your neck are so tense, and your jaw's locked so tight, you're shoving your tone right out into your schnozz. Maybe it sounds great to you, but nobody else likes it." He got his elbows out of the way of an ice bucket. "Free lesson."

The bartender said, "Compliments of the house. You remember Al McDougall, Mr. Meadows?"

"Please leave us alone. Please."

The kid said, "You mean I don't sound good?"

"Well, you make a big sound, but you're making half of it in the wrong place." A girl had come out onto the stage, the one the kid had been talking to, and she was wearing blue corduroy hip-huggers and had painted a tricolored target around her navel. Her long, straight blond hair hung down to her shoulders and spilled over her short pale-blue lace blouse.

Popsy sat up, and she sang:

> *When you've got it made,*
> *What are you made of?*
> *When you've made the grade,*
> *How high are you feeling?*

The combo was backing her lightly but insistently with a fast kind of needling beat, but she was singing it straight and clear.

The kid said, "Yeah, I wanted you to hear her. Rachel Cory."

Popsy shushed him, and the girl sang:

> *How are things on the ceiling?*
> *Can you still see the floor?*
> *Is the daily news a bore*
> *Without your photograph?*
> *Can you still get a laugh*
> *On your side of the mirror?*

She could probably vote, but just barely, and now somebody had come up to their table and Popsy had to rise into a half-crouch in order to see the stage at all.

It was a short squat man saying, "Mr. Meadows, I'd like to introduce—"

"Get the hell out of the way." Popsy gestured at him

with his towel full of crushed ice and saw the line of drop-
lets shoot out of it like holy water. He said, "Sorry, but—"

The kid was standing up. "Mr. Kelly, I'd like you to
meet Popsy Meadows."

"This is a great honor," the man said.

Popsy gave him a wet hand and pulled him gently out
of the way so he could see the stage again.

The man said, "I've taken the liberty of ordering champagne. It would be a great privilege if—"

And he went on talking, but Popsy filtered his voice out
and dumped it aside, along with the kid's replies, and concentrated on the girl who was singing:

> *Do you still sit down*
> *On the same old things*
> *When you dine with kings?*
> *Do you call a spade a spade*
> *Or a heart a heart?*
> *Does that fat heart have wings?*
> *Do the wings have any feathers?*

She was an easy offhanded wonder, she wasn't pushing her
voice or just breathing over the mike the way some of them
did who knew if they ever tried to hit an open note in
middle register they'd sound like Aunt Hattie calling the
boys in for supper.

To the kid, he said, "What's the name of this place?"

"The Finger. Mr. Kelly here—"

The man named Kelly was trying to slide into the booth,
but Popsy got out before he could get trapped, then shoved
the man to the inside. A bartender and a waitress came
fussing up out of the gloom with a champagne bucket and

a bunch of paraphernalia and were getting in the way, and he had to stand up again to see her singing:

> *Do you remember me?*
> *I didn't make the grade.*
> *I got an F in Life*
> *And dropped out of yours.*
> *I'm made of flesh and bone,*
> *And I'm out of fashion,*
> *And that sweet long Cadillac*
> *Is going, going, gone.*
> *Got anything to trade?*
> *Remember kissing me?*
> *Do you still shake hands*
> *Without a rubber glove?*
> *When you've got it made*
> *What are you made of?*
> *Remember anything?*
> *Remember us in love?*

Kelly was saying, "Yes, it's a swell place, and I wouldn't let it go for a cent under—well, I don't even know what I—"

The kid said, "I don't think you should—"

"Though probably you, Mr. Meadows, I mean, having seen them all and coming back to the old tank town, there's no telling what you—"

Somebody put a glass of champagne in Popsy's hand, and he had to drink it in one gulp and put it down so he could clap, then crane his neck and make sure she wasn't leaving the stage yet. While clapping, he apparently backhanded Kelly in the ear because the man yipped and bent sideways. Popsy said, "Sorry," and kept looking.

And now there were more people getting interested in

the booth. During the brief lull, he noticed the general thickening of the heads and shoulders—people from other parts of the club ganging in the aisle between him and the stage—and he knew the symptoms. Under ordinary circumstances, if Sport had been along, he'd have sent him out to get a cab to the back door, but there was nothing ordinary about a birthday any more. His glass was full again, so he drank it.

The kid leaned over Kelly and said, "What I don't get is why you blew into town without any advance men. If we'd known you were coming—"

Kelly said, "If we'd known—"

The kid raised his voice: "—the Mayor would've put on his cowboy hat and electric shorts and—"

Kelly said, "Sure, the Mayor and the Governor would've been—"

The kid tried to be solemn and stay loud at the same time. "Because there's always been a funny feeling around here, you not coming back to your old birthplace even though they kept asking. Everybody figured—"

"They thought maybe you'd make a picture here or something," Kelly said.

The kid said, "There's been some talk, but of course I don't—"

"They think you're stuck up," Kelly said.

The bandage on his upper lip made everything taste like rubbing alcohol, and he tried to push it out of the way without taking it off altogether. The girl was talking over the mike, her hair turning blue and pink under the color wheel, but he couldn't hear what she was saying.

Then the man from the john was back again, smiling

down at him and looking a little beat up around the mouth. "I didn't know it was you, Popsy."

Kelly hollered, "Sam!"

Getting ready to use his elbows on anybody and everybody, Popsy tried to concentrate on the stage.

The kid said, "About once a year some reporter would interview your old man or your old lady and then rehash the same story as before, but they've even quit doing that now. Hell, there was a time you could've been mayor yourself. When I was just a punk—"

The man from the john said, "All you'd a had to do was sing a couple notes, and I'd've known you any place." Then the bartenders had him, and he was going out the hallway backwards.

The combo started again, Popsy said, "Shut up a minute," and the girl sang:

> *Baby, come on inside.*
> *Let's go for a joy ride.*
> *We don't need streets*
> *Or those old red lights,*
> *Just a room*
> *Where it's warm*
> *And nothing else can get in.*

But there was too much talk, and they were spoiling it— the kid putting more ice on his nose between sips of champagne, and Kelly saying, "Well, it's what we all want to do: make a bundle. Right?"

Popsy slid along the seat and stood up, backing into somebody who was trying to talk to him, and he said, "I'll tell you what's in the bundle when you're all finished making it: laundry." They laughed, and someone in the next

78

booth laughed too, and he said, "How about a table near the stage?"

The club was shaped like an oversized diner, and he couldn't see any empty space anywhere. But Kelly and the kid came scrambling out, and then they were barging down the single aisle into a clump of silhouettes who seemed to barge back at them. Popsy got turned sideways in the squeeze till he was facing the booths instead of the stage.

The waitress behind him with the champagne bucket in her arms said, "Gee, I never thought I'd see you in here."

The bandage under his nose tasted more like formaldehyde now, and the girl on the stage sang:

> *Where the sun and the moon*
> *Lie side by side all afternoon,*
> *Where your pearly everlasting body and soul*
> *Are ready to roll . . .*

And there was always a point in a party when things got too loud and too confused and too jumpy, and what had been just indoor sports and current events and good old noise turned into silence, because you couldn't keep track of one sound or one shape long enough to figure it out. It was a time to cruise (because there wasn't much else to do), but it was dangerous too, he recognized threats in it, disasters like broken zippers and blown lines and kicked-out plugs and missed cues and lost scripts and wrong notes, even nonexistent notes, and forgotten appointments and private detectives and dentists.

Kelly was trying to clear a table right in front of the stage, but the people didn't want to get out of it, naturally, and meanwhile back at the ranch, some woman half-sitting

79

in a booth which he was in the process of crushing past had her hand up his crotch in a friendly way, and the man sitting next to her was talking to her about it. The ice bucket was jamming him in the back, and somebody on the other side was trying to pry off his jawline bandage. He was much closer to the girl on the stage now, and there were some flaws in her face, of course, not exactly pockmarks but rough patches, and when he'd gotten himself halfway turned around and mostly disengaged and their eyes met, he could see she was mad about all the racket and jumble during her act. Then someone was shoving a menu at him to autograph, and by the time he'd crumpled it out of the way, the singer was looking somewhere else and Kelly was trying to introduce him to three astonished angry gray-haired men—two of whom were busy brushing spilled drinks out of their laps—and a good-looking college-age girl in a formal, all trapped by the table in the central booth.

Then after a lot of gabble and squeezing, the kid was sitting next to the girl and Popsy had half a haunch on the seat and Kelly was snapping his fingers in the jammed aisle and signaling for a chair.

And the girl on the stage sang:

> *No streetlights, no lightweights,*
> *No wait signs, no fight fans,*
> *No street fights, no breakdowns . . .*

And the other kind of danger in the middle of a first-class muddle was being able to actually understand somebody better than you wanted to. Suddenly out of a solid foot-thick layer of nothing, one voice or one patch of words

80

could stand out with all the stark stupid force of a good slogan. And you had to beware of words hollered or whispered coherently at a long party: they could turn into the wrong kind of dream, could be as haunting as some crappy song a rival singer was pushing too hard. So the best thing to do was to start smearing everything till it all became one big sound like the roar out of an amplifier when the feedback over the mike was full enough.

The kid almost wrecked it right away by being understandable. He said, "What do you want out of this? Which one?" He was leaning close, and the bucket and all the glasses were being reshuffled, and what seemed like hundreds of arms were crossing in front of them and around them, some wanting to shake hands, some wanting to paw. "Which kind?"

Kelly was still bleating for a chair, and then somebody got away with his jawline bandage, and there was a good deal of chatter and happy talk about how nothing was under the bandage. He didn't know whether the girl was still on the stage—the crush up against the table was thicker than ever—and already he was beginning to forget what she looked like.

Over the tops of the other booths, between people who were apparently standing on their seats, he could see part of the front entrance, as inaccessible now as if it had been a doorway on a movie screen. More people were coming through it steadily, and then he caught a glimpse of a hard fast workmanlike knot of TV guys coming through, one with a portable camera hooked over his shoulder, one with a bank of floodlights, and one slapping people out of the way with his notebook.

81

One of the older men at the table shoved a glass of champagne at him and proposed a toast, but Popsy couldn't read his lips, and somebody had hold of his leg under the table, massaging him just above the knee, but he couldn't tell who it was. And it was getting to be about time to shift into overdrive, considering the time, the place, and the decibels. He felt his lungs fill up with air or champagne or spinal fluid or something, and then he was standing on his own seat with the backrest catching him behind the knees and somebody from the next booth trying to hug him from behind.

The noise went up slightly and turned cheerful, and he could see the TV crew wedging its way up the aisle, spreading the mob among barstools on one side and against tables on the other, and somebody swiveled one of the baby spots from the stage right into his face. He staggered slightly from the shock, lost his balance, and had to sit down on top of the backrest, and whoever was hugging him sat down too and started doing a good job of it. She was some kind of woman, he was glad to see, and she kissed him on the cheek and tried to get around far enough to kiss him on the lip bandage. One of her breasts had come out of her low-cut dress, or she'd taken it out in zeal for the commonweal (it wasn't going to get her much publicity, not being one of the standard okay shapes), but the spotlight hadn't had time to follow them down. He stood up again, breaking her grip with his elbows, and Kelly and the kid were helping to brace his legs. He grinned a big one into the harsh blue light, lifted his glass and, with his free hand, stripped the Band-Aid off his lip.

During the cheering he got up on the table, having to

shuffle some glasses out of the way with the edges of his shoes, and now he was almost level with the empty stage four or five feet away. Its emptiness looked beautiful. The bank of floodlights went on, half blinding him, but the cameraman wasn't in position yet; Popsy made gangway gestures at the jam-up of people between him and the stage, and gradually enough of them leaned over backwards to clear a narrow lane. The kid said something and Kelly shrieked something and the table was wobbling under him like a flat-bottomed rowboat. Before it could tilt very much, he went up on his toes and sprang, and he heard the crash behind him at the same time he hit his ankles on the edge of the stage and sprawled forward hard on his hands and knees, losing his glass, which skidded and broke somewhere ahead of him.

He was in the pink part of the color wheel, but then the harsher lights swiveled onto him and he had to keep a good smile going somehow while he scrambled painfully to his feet and felt to see whether his kneecaps were still facing front. They were, and as he straightened up he saw the girl singer sitting on the single step leading up to a door half hidden behind one curtain. She looked nonbelligerent but not exactly friendly. The combo had deserted its instruments on the midget bandstand.

He turned around and held out his hands for silence. Through the glare he could see the table he'd left behind was at least upright though clear of glasses, and everybody everywhere was watching: all the featureless faces were turned toward him, the clumps of heads with colored hair on them, not in orderly rows the way they were in a theater but in swiveling, jerking, and bobbing clusters, most with the red end of a cigarette shining in the middle like a hole burnt through an awning. His feet felt electric, and he knew he had to watch them when they got like that—as if they'd been plugged in and every twitch of a toe, every little shuffle, made very very important noises in his head—and the right side of his brain was doing much better than the left side. Or vice versa. Anyway, he felt as if he'd been crosswired, and it was like trying to comb the hair on the back of his head in a double mirror: he'd signal right and his head would turn left. One of those nights.

Everybody had piped down now, they were waiting for him to do something, so he took the square bandage off his forehead. They cheered. And that was how easy it was sometimes. When they quieted down again, he said, "I'm glad to be back—"

This time they let him have it like a basketball cheering section, but he rode it out with his hands spread for quiet and added, "—but don't worry, I didn't come back to borrow any money." And they laughed like it was the best joke since the invention of the machine gun.

He nodded slowly, let the smile fall, and gave them the serious look from one end of the smoky jumble of a room to the other. The TV camera was up and at him now, and he avoided glancing into its glassy eye. He said, "I only came up here to correct an injustice." He let them think it over for a couple of seconds. "I'm afraid I helped cause a little commotion during a wonderful act, and I want to apologize."

During the applause he offered his hand to the girl, and she got up and tiptoed over through the broken glass and took it without smiling.

He checked her eyes, as blue as the luminous blue eye-shadow she was using, memorized her figure without even seeming to look at it, and said, "I want to reintroduce you to Rachel Cory."

He took the cheering along with her, prolonging it, and he could feel everything good coming back into him, partly through her hand and partly through the crowd and partly through dumb luck and partly up through his spine, out of the old jingle bones. He was in, he was on, he was right, he felt powerful, he could go down into the audience and pick their pockets and squeeze the orange juice out of their daughters and write out a bill of sale for East St. Louis. He could cut up half of them and serve them cold to the other half and they'd ask for more. Why did he ever want any other kind of feeling? Once you'd had that, you weren't really interested in what some chump columnist thought about you or whether the dentist was going to leave you anything in the back row or whether you had an ex-wife or a y-wife or a z-wife on your back. It was burny-burny, bring on the bubbly, open your ears and pull out the cork.

He pointed at the kid, who was sitting with his mouth open at the table below, and made a come-here with one finger.

Into the hand mike the girl said, "Thank you very much, Mr. Meadows. But I finished my act, and I think what the people would like would be to hear something from you."

During the next spate of noise the kid hesitated below the stage, but Popsy came forward and gave him a hand up. He dragged him over to the girl and put an arm around each. A couple of flashguns popped. He said, "And that other great local attraction, Sergio Cantare."

While the people beat their hands together dutifully, Popsy gave the girl a first-class champagne-flight luxury kiss, using up both corners of her mouth. His upper lip was sensitive, even ticklish, where some of the adhesive had lapped over, but he went through with it, hearing the portable camera come humming in for a close-up.

Then, detaching himself, he made a big gesture with both empty arms and said, "I love you, hometowners." He held down the applause with a revival gesture. "After closing time, you're all invited to a party, on me, out at the State Fairgrounds."

They cheered again, and he rode it rapidly backwards and up the step through the stage exit past the combo, who jerked their cigarettes out of his way in the dim narrow corridor. He said, "Go on, back them up," imagining how much better the kid would sound if he had the girl holding his raucous overtones down. He kept going straight through a kitchen the size of a motel room where the smell of deep-frying shut off his wind momentarily, waved at the cooks and waitresses without focusing, turned sideways to bump the panic-bar on a solid metal door, and went stumbling out into a side street before anybody had had time to follow or think to get out the front or out the alley door after him. The good feeling, which he couldn't trust, which he was learning to be scared of, was dwindling fast now and turning screwy, turning mucky in his chest like imitation bronchitis. He started walking.

Are you hungry, Baby? Try me. I'll never tell.
Are you thirsty, Baby? Drop your bucket down my
well.
Make a great big wish and hold it, then go to hell.

Chapter five

When the waitress brought him the 12-inch pizza, he kept both hands over his face as if he were thinking, but he wasn't. She nudged one of his elbows with the plate, making it slide on the tabletop, then went away. The smell of Italian sausage lifted his head to one side, and when he opened his eyes, he was looking at himself in the wall mirror like an interviewer who'd just asked a very very sincere question. But he couldn't think of any sincere answers, nothing straight from the shoulder and off the cuff, nothing from the bottom of his heart. All he felt like doing from the bottom of his heart was throwing up.

The round patch was still on his right cheekbone, and the outside corner of his eye had only puffed a little. He didn't look too bad in the bad light, which was mostly red and blue neon from around the bar's long mirror, but he didn't look particularly familiar.

Out the front window he had a good view of his hotel:

most of the lights on the ninth floor seemed to be turned on. Somebody was waiting up for him, maybe everybody, keeping the home fires burning. He couldn't see any broken windows yet, no smoke coming out, nobody was out on the ledges, and there were no police cars, at least not at the front entrance. All very orderly—he'd have to congratulate Richie and Sport. Then somebody lit the fuse of the juke-box at the back of the bar, and it burst into a loud stereo ruggedy-buggedy piece of hip scat. Keeping a kind of time to it, he began tearing out book matches and sticking them into the pizza with their heads up, one in each piece of sausage and others here and there in the cheese and tomato sauce. He used up more than two books, and by that time the record had quit.

Moving his jaw to get the racket out of his ears and taking his beer with him, he went back to the jukebox and had a look. The few other customers turned or jerked slightly when he went by them, but no one got up, and the bartender was busy washing glasses, and the waitress was having a slow steady comfortable argument with somebody in the kitchen. He didn't know half the names on the list, but the ones he did know were younger than he was, and probably the unknown bunch were too. People were making a habit of being younger.

Only one of his own records was on the board, one out of a hundred, and it wasn't new. He'd cut that three years before—a time so ancient now, he couldn't begin to remember what he'd stuffed in between, all the talk and the women and the wads of dough like insulation. He shoved in a quarter and punched the better side three times and watched the carriage go sliding along the selector board, push him out, put the arm on him, and stick the needle in.

He had a drink of beer and listened to himself just talking on the record, not singing. They'd thought it was a hot idea at the time, and it hadn't done too badly, and if his voice was going to stay down there where his supper was supposed to be, then maybe talking would have to be his *schtik* from now on.

With only a faint kind of muttering groundbeat backing him up, his voice said:

> *You've heard of songs without words.*
> *Well, they're for the birds.*
> *I've got some words without a song.*
> *Hold still, lady.*
> *Hold it steady.*
> *It won't take long.*

But it was only coming out of one speaker at the corner of the glass-fronted metal box. He gave the speaker at the other corner a kick in the slats, but it didn't wake up.

His voice went on steadily, slowly:

> *I couldn't sing this to you if I died trying,*
> *Not even if I were a swan and this was my swan song.*
> *Nothing fouls up a singer worse than crying and crying . . .*

He hit the dead side with the flat of his palm, and the needle jumped in the groove, but nothing else happened.

From behind him the bartender said, "What the hell do you think that is, buddy, a pinball machine?"

He turned and shrugged at the bartender. "One speaker's dead."

"Quit hitting it."

The record went on:

> *So I'll do it this way with a frog in my throat.*
> *I'll do it this way without singing a note.*
> *Maybe you'll understand me better when I say I*
> *love you.*
> *Singing it makes it sound like something coming*
> *from a machine.*
> *Three-for-a-quarter love songs can't say very much*
> *that's new . . .*

The tone arm came off the record, the record went back into its slot, the carriage ran across the letters and numbers, and the same record came out again.

Popsy said, "Hey, it didn't finish." Nobody had pushed the reject button on the back of the machine.

His voice started again, softer than before:

> *You've heard of songs without words . . .*

The bartender said, "If you want it to work, quit kicking it."

"I didn't kick it." Popsy drank some of his beer.

"I *saw* you kick it."

They cut the grooves in a master with the tiny vibration marks that were like the fingerprints of his voice, and then they poured silver over that to make the casting called a *mother*, for godsake, and then they turned him out by the thousands from that mold, just the same as they'd turn out toy soldiers or pocket combs or whatever else they could peddle for enough money in enough places. And finally he wound up spinning in half-busted machines like this, croaking, whooping, and gargling. And it didn't mean a thing.

90

The machine quit in the same place, rejected the record, then put it back on the turntable and started a third time.

The bartender said, "Jesus Christ, buddy, are you trying to wear *every*thing out?"

"I can't help it if it's broken." He slapped the dead speaker once more for good luck, but nothing happened. His voice just skipped a phrase.

"Finish your pizza and get out of here."

He listened to the crackling background of the worn record. The jockeys called that *frying*, and it was a good name for it. He was talking while something was burning. The machine bit him off in the same place, ending with a brief wow as the turntable speeded up and sent his voice from baritone to soprano. He'd been invited to leave, and it was a pleasure. He said, "That's the best suggestion anybody's made all day."

"Never mind the chatter," the bartender said.

Polishing off his beer, he started toward the front but paused at a table where three men and two women were staring at him hard with that it's-him-no-it-isn't look on their faces. He put the empty beer bottle down on its side in the middle of the table and spun it and said, "Somebody's going to have to kiss *some*thing, but it ain't going to be me," and walked away.

His pizza looked like nothing on earth. He lit a match and tried to set fire to the other matches, but he only got a few of them touched off before he burnt his fingers. Looking out the window, he saw the ninth floor was still there, still lit up, and hadn't been pulled out of the hotel like a dresser drawer with mice in it. So he got a handful of change out of his pocket and settled himself in the best seat

91

in the house—in the phone booth near the front door—and pulled out his black book, and gave Gabby a call in Pasadena.

She answered almost right away, and even though he couldn't understand what she was saying, he recognized her bed voice.

He said, "Come on, spit out the cotton. Use words. I can't read sign language over this thing."

She mumbled something else.

He said, "Just to refresh your memory, you've got two lips, one tongue, and two rows of teeth."

"Hello, Popsy." She sounded blurry but all right.

"I won't keep you long," he said. "I want you to meet me."

"I can't."

"What do you mean, you can't? The word's obsolete."

"I'm not going to do it, Popsy. There's a limit."

"Name it."

"I don't want to name anything."

"If the game's got a limit, name it. What's going to make you come? Just name it."

After hesitating and making a noise like a yawn, she said, "I won't. I forget the names of things."

"Is he there?"

"Is who here?"

Popsy tried to remember. "Him. You know."

"There isn't any him. I quit all that. I swore off. Even my cat makes the place seem crowded."

A couple of people came by the phone booth to look in at him, and he wedged the door open with his foot to shut off the light. He said, "A tomcat?"

"Why not? You think I want a bunch of kittens lapping it up around here?"

He let her have a little breezy sincerity. "Come on, it'll only take you a little while. I'm in San Francisco at the St. Francis. Fly up. Fifth floor, name of Spencer."

"Fly on what?"

"On an airplane."

She said, "I'm broke till the end of the month."

He caught a familiar flicker out of the corner of his eye, and when he focused through the glass on the TV set perched on a wall shelf, he was on it, looking big and easy on the small stage with the girl singer next to him. He said, "Fly now, pay later. I'll pay you back."

"I'm too scared of you. That's the honest-to-God truth. Something's the matter with you."

"With *me*? Am *I* living alone with a cat?" Now he was introducing the kid and kissing the girl, and the camera came bobbing in for a close-up.

"I don't know. What *are* you doing?"

"I'm exercising my soul in a hotel room."

"It could use some exercise."

Now the news announcer was on, saying something and smiling and shaking his head. Then his high-school non-graduation picture came sliding onto the screen with a faraway serious look on its face, the result of a half pint of whiskey he'd substituted for lunch on a bet that day. He said, "Okay, so come on and exercise it."

"I didn't like your last record."

"Thanks."

"I thought I'd better say so. It's sort of squawky, as if you were mad and wanted to cut somebody up."

"Don't tell *me* about cutting up." Then there was a picture of him in a football uniform with his helmet under his arm and his hair curling onto his forehead. He turned his eyes away quickly because anything could be next, and he wasn't ready for it.

"Let's just forget it, Popsy. We don't have it any more, and even if we had it, I wouldn't want it. You're like a sausage machine, and I've already been through once."

He said, "Aw, baloney."

"Ha, ha, ha."

He gave the operator some more money, then said, "What're you doing right now?"

"I'm in my pajamas and I'm trying to get up enough energy to go back to sleep."

She didn't sound completely sure about it, and he stole another look at the TV in time to see himself holding a pair of oversized boxing gloves between his grim-looking face and his old man's smiling angular profile. His old man's gloves were much smaller and, he remembered, much harder. In the phone booth his chin buried itself instinctively in his shoulder for protection.

She said, "What're you grunting about?"

"How much do you want?"

"I told you I'm broke. If you were broke, how much would *you* want?"

For years he'd dreamed of being able to hit his old man back, but as soon as he got big enough to do it, the game had changed. He said, "Well, come on up, and you can have a grand."

In a practical voice she said, "Wire it to me."

"I can't. I don't want anybody to know where I am for a few days. I need a rest and I need you."

"Let Sport send it."

And then his mother was taking up the whole screen with a head-shot from younger days, her face looking like one of her own pies when the juice had bubbled out of the slits a little too much. One of the women from the spin-the-bottle table suddenly appeared on the other side of the sliding door, peering in at him. He said, "Don't be so edgy. Come on up and you can have it."

"Separate from alimony."

"Sure, sure."

"Cash."

"Cash."

"It'll take me a while to get in the mood. Anybody else there?"

Another woman's head came and joined the first, getting in the way of the TV. They both had stringy hair, and their red mouths were taking turns chattering into each other's ears, and he could see them touching themselves constantly and lightly, making sure hair, earrings, necklaces, bras, hemlines, and seams were in the right places. If they'd had time, they might have brushed their teeth and taken another lesson at modeling school or had another fanny-belt session at the reducing parlor. He said, "No, nobody else."

"Will I need a lot of clothes?"

"Absolutely no."

She chuckled, imitating her old seductive voice. "My, my. At your age. Happy birthday."

"On my birthday I wear my birthday suit. Thanks for remembering."

"My lawyer isn't going to like this."

"Shall I send him a bag of groceries?"

95

"No."

The women had backed off a little now, still talking, and he could see the announcer again and then the shot of a building on fire with firemen hosing it and climbing up ladders. He said, "The St. Francis, fifth floor, Spencer."

"All right, Popsy. Be nice to me."

"It's a deal." He hung up before she did, then slid the door open and sat waiting.

The women came up, shoulder to shoulder, and the taller one said, "Oh, Mr. Meadows, take us to your party. It sounds like fun."

"Which party?"

"The one out at the Fairgrounds. It was just on TV."

"Tell you what." He sat straight in the booth, feeling like a priest in a confession box. "Meet me there in an hour in the cattle barn. You know where they show the bulls?"

Excitedly the shorter one said, "We'll find it. Those aren't our husbands over there."

He kept his voice cool and didn't look at them. "Which one of you likes it the most?" He felt a tremendous weariness.

There was an embarrassed silence during which the two women took turns not quite meeting each other's eyes. Then the taller one said, "I do."

"What?" The shorter one looked shocked.

Their two escorts were standing up at the table but apparently hadn't decided to come over yet, and Popsy pretended to glance the taller woman up and down. "Which ways do you like it best?"

The shorter one backed off a couple of steps, and after

shaking her head briefly as if to clear it, the taller one said, "That's for you to find out."

He stood up. "Say three Hail Mary's and two Our Father's, and I'll see you on Sunday." The women were under thirty, but not by much, and he felt some strange emotion toward them. Something abstract with a capital letter at the front of it.

The taller one said, "Which cattle barn?"

He gave them his tired but happy exit, the sideways, genial, sacrificial, sweating, deep-breathing, nodding, it's-all-for-you shuffle, and went out the front door into the warm night, and started for the hotel. The Fairgrounds would be a good place for everyone to get together, all the ones who didn't want to go home if there was anything else going on; and though he wouldn't be able to make it himself in person, there would be plenty of last year's sawdust and bullshit in case they wanted to make their own host, plenty of raw material.

And he made it through the swinging doors and halfway through the lobby before two sleepy-looking reporters had jerked themselves up out of a sofa and started hanging questions on him like ornaments. All he gave them was a stream of hello's and glad-to-see-you's, and he bent far over the counter to catch the night clerk by the lapel of his plaid vest and whisper, "Did Sport take care of you?"

The clerk nodded, and the reporters were trying to jam in close to hear, and Popsy held out his hand. "I want a list of the rooms we're in now, and I want a key that works them all."

The clerk said, "We can't give out passkeys."

One of the reporters said, "How many are in your party, Mr. Meadows?"

Locating a couple of twenties in his pocket, Popsy stuffed them inside the clerk's vest, then waited while he went to a room behind the mailboxes. For the first time, he noticed the uniformed cop standing beside the elevator, hands behind him, big smile on his pink face.

The other reporter said, "What's the reason for your visit?"

"Business."

"Show business?"

"All business is connected: show business, monkey business, big business, giving somebody the business, political business. It's an interlocking network." The clerk handed him a piece of paper wrapped around a key, and he headed for the elevator.

The first reporter said, "Any truth to the rumor that you're planning to enter the primary for mayor?"

"In my business, the job seeks the man. Is it empty?" The cop pushed the button for him, and the elevator door opened. He stepped in.

The second reporter said, "Any romance brewing?"

"I'm always open for suggestions." At the last moment before the doors closed, the cop gave a little two-finger salute, then braced the door with a foot and an elbow long enough to let a bellhop squeeze in, carrying two big paper bags with liquor bottles sticking out of the tops. Popsy said, "What floor, as though I didn't know."

"Nine."

He punched that number on the automatic board and had time to read the list of rooms before they got there—

six of them now, which wasn't too bad, considering—and only two of them marked as suites. Then he took a bottle of bourbon from the nearest sack and said, "It's okay, I'm paying for it anyway."

The bellhop said, "I know."

"Do you collect stamps?" He tried to peel off the tax stamp, but when it broke and the bellhop said no, he went ahead and pulled the cork and rinsed the beer out of his mouth. "Is it a good party?"

The elevator stopped at the ninth floor, and the bellhop said, "I don't know, Mr. Meadows. I haven't seen all of it. It's sort of hard to see."

In the hall there was another uniformed cop and no particular action, and he got out a twenty and prepared to stick it into the long claw of the law, but the cop was grinning at him, so he held back.

The cop said, "Hi, Popsy. Remember me?"

"No." He followed the bellhop to the door where most of the noise was coming from.

"I used to tend bar at your old man's place."

He gave him the twenty out of force of habit and said, "If you see any suspicious characters out here, salute." Because there were bound to be suspicious characters. Nobody was creeping down the corridors at the moment, but if somebody didn't get busy soon, he'd do it himself.

The bellhop knocked at the door, and the cop said, "Your old man's just as ornery as ever. Lost a little weight."

Popsy pressed the bottle against his stomach and felt annoyed, and then Richie opened the door and started making bird noises, flapping his elbows. Popsy poured a welcoming drink down his own throat and shut the cop off

99

in the middle of a life sentence and kept the bellhop to flavor the party a little. It looked like Scene Ten, the Drunken Debauch, Vintage 1941, with some fairly young women he didn't recognize and Mary-Mary telling a young man an old story in the corner and Sport playing the piano and the smoke thick enough to cut up into souvenirs. He got a kind of general howdy from six or eight places in the room.

Popsy said, "How's it going?"

Richie's eyes looked fogged, and he kept trying to take up the slack at both sides of his mouth. He said, "I'm wilted. Cast aside like a rose under the balcony after the beautiful broad has listened to the serenade and chucked her lunch."

"Get another writer." Popsy helped himself to another drink and felt the buzzing start in the left side of his head. It was like the buzz of an electric alarm clock, and he was supposed to get up and do something, but he couldn't remember what it was. There were no strings on his fingers and, when he looked, no notes in his pockets.

A girl disentangled herself from the bunch near the piano and came weaving up to him, laughing helplessly. She looked vaguely familiar, but too vaguely, and she had some kind of dip-stick with a looped handle stuck down her cleavage inside her orange jersey.

She said, "Check my oil. I want to see how oiled I am."

Richie pulled it out and pretended to taste the end of it. "You're down a quart." He put it back carefully, and she reeled away, telling everyone what he'd said.

Popsy found himself beginning to talk to a lot of people, not exactly on purpose, but he'd start to talk to one—just to get it straight who he was or she was (you have to learn people's names or they think you don't care, and as a general rule all women are called honey and all men are called pal, occasionally Susan and Fred) because if he was going to give a party, he wanted to *give* it—and before he'd even gotten the name business fixed up, somebody else would join in, and a third, and there'd be three names to forget instead of just one. And then seven names in a circle, and he'd be telling them about something that happened to him ten years ago—what he'd said to somebody, for instance—and they'd all start whooping and clutching and changing positions so the names weren't in the right order any more anyway, and there was no use trying to remember. He also had a sort of enjoyable tendency to talk loud because when you have a good voice you might as well use your God-given attribute at every convenient opportunity, allowing full scope to the trilled, lateral, and fricative consonants and putting the burrs and the cleats on the edges of the best words. This didn't necessarily interfere with the music, though he could see Sport giving him a reproachful eye over the top of the piano once in a while, but usually in the fullness of time—and time had seldom been fuller—he felt loaded with good ideas, none complete but all perfectly clear; and if you were trying to explain a really rich idea to a guy like Richie, you didn't want the mixer at the control panel turning up the piano too high and you didn't want a lot of walla-walla from the mob. You needed elbow room and floor space and a cardioid mike you could talk into from anywhere except behind.

He poured himself another drink without using a glass and said something funny to Richie. He could tell it was funny because Richie laughed so hard he broke something loose in his chest and had to cough it up in a handkerchief. Then Popsy crossed the room and said something funny to Mary-Mary, and she started telling him one about the Hollywood producer who felt lousy all the time and finally went to the doctor. He began saying something else funny, and she raised her voice and said the doctor couldn't find anything wrong at all and asked the producer to describe a typical working day in detail in case he was doing something detrimental to his health. He asked the young man with Mary-Mary what his name was, and Mary-Mary raised the producer's voice to the edge of blasting and said, "I get up about 7 a.m. and go in the bathroom and throw up, then shave—I use an electric razor—and throw up, then I take a shower and get dressed and throw up, then I read the paper and have a glass of tomato juice and throw up, and by this time my chauffeur is out front to take me to the studio, and I get to my office by eight sharp and have coffee and toast and throw up, and then I—" And she interrupted herself with the doctor's deep voice and said, "Wait a minute. You mean you do this every day? You get up and throw up and so on?" Popsy shook hands with the young man, forgetting his name immediately, and Mary-Mary turned the producer's voice on full again and said, "Why, yes. Doesn't everybody?"

She laughed harder at her own joke than she'd laughed at his, which was her privilege, of course, but not exactly shrewd when you came right down to it. He went over and said something pretty funny to Alice, who had appeared from one of the other rooms and was looking happy and frazzled. He started to listen to her explain something im-

102

portant but it wasn't very interesting, so he listened to a couple of the expensive-looking girls who had probably fallen through the ceiling or come through the ventilator, but they only lasted about a sentence and then they wanted *him* to say something. He couldn't think of anything right away, so he had a drink. Then there was a sort of lap dissolve from here to the other side of the room behind the piano, and he was talking to Warbucks Buxton, whose hairpiece was hanging sideways over one temple now, and it was all about this and that and whatnot and where the next money was coming from in case anybody wanted to know. Sport kept giving him stings on the piano like music cues, but he wasn't having any of that. He was having a good time even though he felt terrible. Or maybe he was having a terrible time even though he felt good.

He had the idea of going over to the best-looking girl in one of the loud corners and seeing how her breasts were, and he did and they were all right: real and perfectly matched, as far as he could tell by sight alone. She turned him halfway out of the group and said something serious to him which he didn't catch and he said something funny which she laughed at. There seemed to be a good deal of coming and going through all the doors he could focus on, and that was okay as far as it went, but then one of the people was Kitch Steinway, his business manager, looking small, disgusted, flatfooted, neat, tired, and half-stoned.

He said, "Kitch, I had enough sense not to call you. What the hell are you doing here?"

"I heard you calling me in my brain. Without a phone."

Richie came up and said something which wasn't funny, and Kitch smiled which was typical, and Popsy pointed at

103

Kitch and said, "I know you, you're the voice of reason, and you can go play yourself a chorus on the sloop whistle. This is a birthday party and we're blowing our minds."

Kitch said something reasonable and Richie goosed him, and then Kitch said, "Okay, okay, what do you want?" He spread his hands. "Am I an enemy? If we get sued, I want to be here to see why."

Popsy said, "I'll tell you what: quit standing on the carpet."

"On the carpet?"

"Yes, get off the carpet. Some poor family in Syria or Turkey or some place spent half their lives sewing up this carpet, and—"

Kitch said, "This is the second-best nylon pile from probably Burlington."

"They mix the dye with yak butter instead of eating their square meals, and finally they sell the thing for enough dough to get buried on, and guys like you come shuffling around and standing on it and spilling your drinks—"

"Who's spilling?"

So Popsy spilled his drink for him, then poured them both another—his own into his mouth where it was more convenient to carry, less liable to make rings on the tables. If the method was good enough for squirrels (he swallowed half and kept half in his cheek pouch), then it was good enough for him.

One of the young leather-faced guys had started to sing at the piano—a slurpy, slidy, syrupy version of some very popular piece of country blues which he himself hadn't cut yet—and he put a stop to it by walking right up to the

104

guy and taking a good look inside the mouth at the capped teeth and the shrinking tongue. And it wasn't the first time it had occurred to him that he'd been opening his big mouth in front of crowds for thirty years or more and that, if you didn't bother to listen, a man singing looked like a man drowning. Somebody under fifty feet of water. Or like a man falling off a bridge or out of an airplane. A good high note and a scream looked just the same on the face, used the same muscles, made it just as hard to keep the eyes open, and whatever kind of noise was coming out of the mouth—the invisible snake with its scales barbed backwards, an extrusion of plastic pulp, a coiled-spring cloth-covered jack-in-the-box, or an old-fashioned hand-painted canvas panorama with scenes of Grand Canyon and Yosemite Falls and other natural wonders, or giant voice balloons with sweet heart-gripping words etched on them forever and ever, the words about the simple things of life, the three little words, or the great big brassy hog-calling circus-lettered streamers made out of white butcher paper announcing the arrival of that equally great big feel-ing, Me Doing Something to You. Or else it was the scream falling off the bridge or deep underwater, a song with no lyric, but heartfelt and memorable. The face was the same.

And after he'd shut the young man's face, he shut his own for a while, keeping the drink stored in one side of it till it burned the lining too much or maybe dissolved a few teeth and leaked inside and went down to join the others. Somebody put some records on, and Sport left the piano, and then there was a fade-out and a fade-in, and he was looking at himself with one eye in the bathroom mirror, checking the red puff of damage under the bandage on his cheekbone. And the girl standing behind him was Miss Armory looking as though she'd been aimed at and hit, the sequins all pointing the wrong way up her bulging front. He had another drink of something which he seemed to have in his hand, and then there was a lap dissolve back to the big room and he was making an announcement.

It seemed very popular with the few people left, and he got down on his hands and knees and started cutting up his blue sportcoat with a pair of manicure scissors. He had to go slow because the material clogged the blades, but he worked up the back far enough so he could rip it into a bunch of strips which he then cut crossways into smaller strips six inches long. He stuck one finger securely through the hole in a roll of adhesive tape and collected the most judicious-looking people left in the room, rejecting all the youngest as being too frivolous to be trustworthy and dubbing Kitch his second-in-command. And then with a flourish of his arms he let himself be helped out into the hall past the policeman, who kept his feet planted right where they were and gave everybody a big crooked smile, and down to the next door and through it with the passkey into the darkness where he was the first but not the last to bump into the bed. And as soon as somebody turned the overhead light on, he began to announce the first winner of the Greater Fowler County Purebred Livestock and Home-cooking Fair, which turned out to be Warbucks in a T-shirt and some unknown quantity in a necklace, to whom he presented after a brief talk the Atomic J. Lamplighter Artificial Insemination Award. He taped one of the blue flannel ribbons to the nearest part of Warbucks and went through the half-open connecting door into the near-dark again and found flat-chested Theresa in something that looked like boxer's shorts. She was dragging a sheet over a lump the size of a curled-up human being, and when the others came bumping in behind Popsy, she came groggily up to her knees on the bed, ready to fight, and without further fanfare he gave her the Popsy Meadows Award for her tireless efforts in Lactation Research among the Udders of Underage Holstein Heifers with oakleaf clusters (to be given later) and he taped the ribbon on the lump.

Because if a lot of townspeople were going to be having a good time out at the Fairgounds in the middle of the night, it was only right and fitting that he inject a little ceremony into his own scene. And they had to go out by way of the corridor again before he could let everybody into the next room with the passkey, and he taped another ribbon on the broad bare back of Chris Michelson before he could get the bathroom door shut behind him, and then Popsy had to give him the short spiel through the door, presenting him with the Indoor Open All-State Cross-bred Swine Cup. Somebody left a highball glass on the floor, and Popsy explained how they'd have the handles glued on later and the whole thing spruced up. They couldn't find anybody else in the room, not even out the window, so they went through the connecting door, having to give the bolt a little persuasion, and they turned up the lights on Alice the Foaming Cleanser who was passed out between a half-dressed young man and a half-dressed young woman, her own ragged white gown looking like a tablecloth after a convention banquet, and it gave him great pleasure to present her with the King Farouk Award for Landrace-Hampshire Inbred Sows.

And then they had to go out into the corridor again, and there seemed to be more members of the Judges' Committee than before, but he didn't slow down to count them because he was busy trying to check the right numbers on the doors: the piece of paper the night clerk had given him was soaking wet, and some of the numerals had gone blurrier than others. But he didn't let that stand in the way of progress, and he let everybody into the corner suite where a fat man and a fat woman came bolting up out of twin beds and blinking at the light. They didn't look like legitimate entries, but he presented them with blue ribbons in the Indeterminate Sex Division of the Mixed Pickle and Potted Beef Contest and let it go at that, there were plenty of ribbons, and then they all got out, after receiving directions about how to do it, and he let them in the next door where the girl who'd had the dip-stick down her front was trying to get one of the slick young guys out of the shower stall in one piece. Her negligee was soaked all the way down the front, so Popsy had to tape the ribbon on one swaying shoulder blade as he gave her the Unwed Mothers' Lattice-top Cherry Tart Contest Award, and he tucked another ribbon under the young man's sagging lower lip and let it hang down like a tongue as he honored him with the Star Milker Award of the American Billygoat Association.

And then they were out in the hall again, and he was in the middle of presenting a special award to Kitch for his unbiased silence, when suddenly he started thinking about something else. He gave himself a drink to make it go away, but it didn't. Instead, he went away.

Let it go, Baby, you know what it's all about.
Take the top off the bottom, pour the sauer off the
   kraut.
It was straight last night, this morning it's inside out.

Chapter six

He broke out of a bad sleep like a man coming up out of a
submarine disaster, rising with the help of a huge bubble
full of smoke, debris, and the yowls of the ones who hadn't
made it yet, who might never make it, and when he hit the
surface, stunned and bobbing around and kicking at the
sheets, he couldn't be sure what might come up under
him at any moment—sharks, fuel oil, pieces of people—but
he could tell already it wouldn't be anything good.

There was a mound beside him on the bed, completely
buried under a tangle of blankets and sheets and one omi-
nous oversized empty brassière which rode the top of the
heap like some kind of busted radar equipment. He re-
coiled and just saved himself from sliding out onto the floor
by ramming his crazy-bone into a half-open bedstand
drawer. Pausing there with one foot on the carpet, he cased
the room: he was still in the hotel, but whether it was his
own room or not, he couldn't tell without digging into the

closet or the bathroom, and he didn't want to wake up the heap by any sudden moves. For godsake, the heap was as big as he was—or was that just a trick of the blankets? Hardly anybody wore a brassière that big. Maybe it was a trophy from some other room, some other encounter in the middle of the night, maybe it had been like bringing back a record spread of kudu horns.

Nausea wasn't hitting him yet, but he could feel it waving at him from underneath, ready to come pouring up and take over the minute he gave it the least sign of recognition. He braced his elbow hard on the bedstand and eased himself out farther, and it was like failing a strength test in a gym class: he couldn't keep from joggling the mattress again and again while he got his other foot on the floor. And the heap shifted and stirred, grunted, then let out a moan, a kind of croaking, ragged, splintery, deeply experienced baritone moan that nobody under forty can make, and he got out of the bed in a hurry now (he was stark naked!), shifting his raw eyes around the room in an unsuccessful hunt for clothes and/or anything else he could possibly wear. The drapes were only open about a foot and a half, but there was enough bleak morning light to see a pair of pants by, and he couldn't. He steadied himself against the wall and suddenly tasted brass, thick and strong like some kind of warning, like a notice from his stomach that the vaults were going to fly open and let all the dead money out, and when he tried to move his tongue, it ran into an obstruction between the outside face of his teeth and the wall of his cheek, as if all his fillings had run over into one side of his mouth during the night. He fished it out, and it was the passkey.

The heap was stirring again, and he took a quick peek into the closet—nothing in it, nothing at all except a couple of paper laundry bags which he could wear like overshoes maybe or over his head. So that meant it wasn't his own room; retreating to the no-exit safety of the bathroom would be silly. The wall-to-wall carpeting was nailed down, the drapes looked too sturdy to pull down without a wrestling match, therefore he'd have to snatch one of the sheets or a blanket from the mess on the bed, unless he wanted to chance a nude dash through the corridor—it would make a good spread in *Life* or *Playboy*, depending on the angle a photographer might catch him, or maybe a three-color cover on *Jaybird, The Sunshine Magazine*. One of the green blankets looked fairly loose—at least it didn't disappear into any noticeable crevices—and he got a good grip along its whole bottom edge and gave it a sudden large-scale yank on the general principle of a magician he'd once seen in a nightclub act who could whisk the table-cloth from under a full-course dinner for two without spilling the shrimp cocktails.

It didn't exactly work, but he got the blanket and had time to halfway wrap himself up in it before the large dreadful smeared groggy face of Mary-Mary came rearing up out of the heap with one of its eyes open.

He said, "Oh, no." He realized he was talking to himself, but the responsible part of him wasn't there to answer.

One of Mary-Mary's breasts came out in the open too, lolling over the edge of the sheet like the end-product of some foolhardy experiment in the hybridization of gourds and jellyfish. For a moment, he couldn't take his eye off it, and vice versa, and then Mary-Mary said, "Oh, hi, baby."

There was no connecting door, so he headed for the outside, trying to think of something polite to say to her and not making it. If he tried to talk now without wetting his lips, they'd split, and he didn't want to touch his lips with his tongue or his face with his hands or anything else with anything else.

She said, "Hey!" when he went out the door into the corridor and bumped his way among the groups of men standing around smoking and gabbing toward what seemed more or less like the right door. He pulled the blanket up over his head like a cowl, crouched, and even though he felt sick, he kept his eyes on the right spot and his elbows out like a blocking guard and got the passkey into the knob on the third try while the men behind and ahead of him were just beginning to holler and use his name in vain. Either the corridor cops had sprung a leak or somebody had decided to pay them more than Sport, but he couldn't worry about that now, not having enough undamaged brain tissue to concentrate on anything but getting the door bolted behind him and getting himself around the corner into the recovery room—after a quick bed-check to make sure he wasn't going from bad to worse, though anything worse than Mary-Mary, at least for shock value, would have to be invented by a good makeup department.

He shut himself into the bathroom. It was the right one, thank God, and nobody, not even himself, had looted it or played pigsty in it during the night. Letting the blanket fall, he gave his hands and face a preliminary wash, then took aspirin and a tranquilizer. He avoided the mirror completely, but as he washed his hands in the bowl, he felt like a doctor after some kind of operation. Yet he felt like the patient too, and he had to suppress the standard dialogue that streamed through his head—How am I? Am I going to live? Did I make it? Did everything come out all right? *Don't worry about a thing. Try to get some rest. Congratulations, it's a boy.* Suddenly he felt like crying, which he'd always heard was the healthiest way to celebrate a birthday, but there was nobody there to swat him on the behind and he felt too weak to reach it himself.

After a shower and a shave, he'd just begun to establish the idea that he might live, when Sport knocked and said, "The Mayor's here."

He didn't answer, not being able to think of anything worth the effort.

Sport rattled the knob. "You in there? The Mayor's here."

"Tell him I want ten across the board on Mr. Death in the Second at Saratoga."

"The Mayor. With a delegation, some of which are pissed off and some of which aren't. What's all this about the Fairgrounds?"

Getting on a clean pair of shorts without falling over, he unbolted the door, brushed Sport out of the way, and tried to remember where the closet was. "What happened to you last night?" It was always a good defensive opening, just in case Sport had done anything wrong.

"As soon as I got my blue ribbon, I hit the hay. I figured I couldn't improve on an honor like that."

"What'd I give it to you for?" He found a new pair of slacks, and then Sport was holding a crisp unbuttoned shirt open for him. He lost track and tried to do both at once

113

and found himself barging forward into the closet, ringing a cluster of empty hangers together.

"If you don't remember, that's fine."

He steadied himself and got his arms all the way through the sleeves before trying to pull up the slacks. "Mayor who? What the hell does he want?"

"Ormond Haggis. He told me five times and spelled it twice."

"Oh, for godsake." Popsy raised his zipper very slowly and steadily in spite of the shock. It was a lesson he'd learned the hard way on bad mornings. "My old football coach. They finally got rid of him."

"And what do you mean, what does he want?" Sport said. "What does any mayor want?"

While Sport did his cuff links, he let his eyes close and tried to get a little more sleep, but the idea of his old rotten coach as mayor was too good: he wanted to stay awake for it. "Can't you get them to come back later? I'm not exactly warmed up yet."

"I don't think so. He's in the next room with a secretary, and it was all I could do to keep the whole gang from coming in—I mean, like the City Council and guys like that—because the wreckage is pretty thick in there. I got most of the bottles out, but—"

"Okay, okay."

"And I don't think the Council likes standing in the hall much."

"There's a bar downstairs. I didn't invite the bastards."

Sport threaded a necktie under the collar and began tying it. "Kitch says you're in a little trouble and to act nice."

"He says that every time anybody winds him up."

114

"How's your memory?"

He avoided Sport's eye and tried to make the brassy bloody taste go out of his mouth by sheer willpower. "Compared to whose? If you were sacked out, how's *your* memory? I remember what I remember. If that isn't all, that's the way it goes."

"Don't get mad."

He sat down and closed his eyes during the rest of the operation—the socks, the shoes—and Mary-Mary started to come back to him. She was dancing or at least jiggling, and then he seemed to be dancing too which was impossible: he couldn't possibly have danced in the nude with Mary-Mary, except maybe for some very important private joke, or he would never speak to himself again.

Sport said, "You didn't exactly part your hair in the right place."

"Leave it alone, it's good enough for them." He focused on the top of the dresser crowded with empty bottles. "Is there anything to eat in there? Coffee?"

"Yes."

He got off the edge of the bed. "Did Belle call?"

"The phone was so screwed up, I couldn't tell whether the calls were coming or going. One of the switchboard girls was up here half the night, and—"

"Never mind, never mind." He headed for the connecting door. "Let's see what this jerk wants." He went into the other room, located the breakfast table, and got to it without stopping or changing direction or shifting his eyes, and by the time he'd settled himself, Haggis was already talking.

Popsy stuffed a piece of toast into his mouth so he wouldn't have to think right away and looked the man over: he'd put on weight, and his gut was thicker than his chest now, as thick as his shoulders were wide, silver hair, sunburned face with a big mouthful of white stubby teeth, obviously real. He was shaking hands over the table and introducing his secretary, a slim small dark-eyed number with no makeup. His voice was blaring and cheery and phony, and it made Popsy's head hurt.

Haggis said, "I knew we'd get you back into town. After all these years." To his secretary: "My star half-back." Then soberly toward the piano: "We've both changed our sphere of activity. Assumed other responsibilities."

Then there was a pause, during which Popsy knew he was supposed to say something philosophical. He chewed his toast, and it tasted like a piece of blanket.

Haggis said, "We've both of us learned and believed in a combination of team play and individual initiative, all aimed at the common good. That's why I'm sure you'll take this in a spirit of—"

"What's good about losing a football game?" Popsy's voice felt muddy and he coughed some toast out of it.

"It isn't whether you win or lose, it's how you play the game." Haggis said it seriously.

"How about those gouges and that elbow stuff you taught us? I suppose that's—"

Topping him and making a broad gesture with one broad hand, Haggis said, "That's why I'm sure you'll take my suggestion in the spirit it's offered. As you may have heard we had a little trouble at the Fairgrounds last night—I won't go so far as to call it a riot, that's an exaggeration you can expect from newspapers—but it wasn't funny, and five people including three policemen had to be treated at the hospital. Seems there was a rumor about a big Popsy Meadows party, and they've got barbed wire on top of the hurricane fence out there, and—"

"Well, it's understandable how something like that got started. Some people talk." Popsy tried to look blandly at Sport, but moving his head made everything turn yellow in the corners of his eyes, and he quit. "We had a little party here at the hotel. A birthday party."

"I heard about it. I've seen some of the damage too, and I've heard the stories of some respectable citizens whose rooms were invaded in the middle of the night by—they had trouble describing the gang." Haggis smiled like a coach who's just seen a very sloppy tackle by his own team. "No, the rumor got started by a public announcement over TV, and you'd be surprised how many people believed it."

"It was a joke." He inhaled some steam from a cup of coffee, but didn't venture to drink it.

"I've heard better."

Popsy said, "Where's Kitch?"

Sport started to say something, but Haggis said, "I've deliberately asked Mr. Steinway to stay out of this for the time being, so you and I could get reacquainted on a personal unofficial level. I have a proposition."

He sipped at the coffee warily. "As I understand the word *proposition*, somebody usually gets screwed at the end of it. No thanks. I've taken enough of that from you. By the way, how the hell did you ever get to be mayor? Somebody must've really been—"

"Let's stick to business, Popsy."

"Okay, Gut. What's the secretary for if this is private?"

Haggis broadened his smile. "People don't call me Gut any more."

"Why not? They've got twice as much reason."

Slowing down and speaking calmly, Haggis said, "The secretary's in case we need a record of anything. You can see she isn't writing yet."

"What's your name again, honey?"

The secretary said, "Stella Chambers."

And he heard the way she said it. He looked Haggis over as carefully as his eyes would let him. "Does Miss Chambers do quite a bit of traveling with you?"

"No." Haggis flushed. "She happens to be a friend of my wife's."

"How would you *like* to do some traveling, Miss Chambers?"

Raising his voice, Haggis said, "Let's get down to business. As you probably know, our annual Cornflower Festival starts tomorrow. And to put matters in a nutshell, we'd like you in the parade. Up front."

Popsy sipped more coffee. "With you. In an open car."

"Well, we hadn't gotten that far in the arrangements yet, but—"

"Sport and I were talking about it earlier. What does any mayor want? He wants to get reelected, he wants to look good, he wants more of what's going around, and he doesn't want to get caught—not necessarily in that order. How many did I get right?"

Using more and more of a public voice, Haggis said, "I think it's the least you can do for your hometown after years of neglect, then making so much trouble and sending people to the hospital."

118

Popsy leaned forward over his tray, then had to turn his head away from the odor of scrambled eggs. "Tell me, Gut, were you really getting into that French teacher or did you just spread the rumor yourself?"

"There's a lady present. I know show-business morals are supposed to be lax, but—"

"Where'd you learn to say things like that, Gut? Remember what you used to say to those lady gym teachers who stayed on the basketball court too long? You'd put your hand in your pants and say—"

"Never mind!" Haggis shifted from the arm to the deep seat of an easy chair and collected himself like a dealer who'd just spilled a deck of cards. "Old friends can always remember unflattering things about each other, whether they're true or not. Don't get me started. Every now and then a magazine asks me to remember something about you."

Sport said, "I'd better call Kitch."

"No." Haggis smiled. "Let's forget about the bygones. I don't know whether I can arrange national publicity, but both the local TV stations will cover it, and that means statewide, you can have a key to the city if you feel like it, and there's a new recreation area that needs naming. *Meadows Park* not only sounds dignified but natural."

"*Popsy Park* isn't bad either." He waved at Sport to sit down.

"Well, I—" Haggis turned to Miss Chambers. "What do you think?"

"I think he's kidding, sir."

Popsy said, "How about an honorary degree from my old high school?"

"If that's a serious request, I'll see what I can do. But it

119

isn't the right season and it doesn't sound very—uh, dignified. Our City College may not be very well known, but it's perfectly capable of conferring honorary degrees."

"My old man still runs a bar out on the edge of town."

Haggis nodded. "A popular place, I understand, but it's not on the edge any more. We've been undergoing what's known as urban sprawl."

"How would you like to have this whole deal set up and the cameras grinding and the City Council all lined up with their bellies hanging out and cornflowers stuck behind their ears, and then I haul back and give my dear old seventy-five-year-old dad a sock right in his big fat mouth?"

Haggis shrugged. "That's up to you. As long as you don't try it on me, in which case my police bodyguard would have to deal with you the way old Schwartz used to take care of you on that off-tackle slant."

Popsy looked him over for a while, enjoying the size of everything—as long as they were going to make a Haggis, they might as well have made a big one—and the purity of the expression on the square face. Then he said, "Gut, how would you like me to run against you for mayor?"

"I wouldn't. Luckily for me, if you ever announced anything like that, the boys would have you talked into running for governor or senator instead in five minutes. Want to try? Be a treat to have five first ladies or however many it is."

Even though it hurt his ears to smile, Popsy tried it on one side. "Miss Chambers, why don't you take the rest of the day off?"

She said, "I'd love to."

"Now, wait a minute," Haggis said.

"I'll have some oysters sent up."

She was on the only straight chair in the room, and she sat up straight in it, her toes just touching the floor. "Well, if it's all right with Mayor Haggis—"

"Cut it out." Haggis didn't even bother to look at her. "So shall I send in the chairman of the Arrangements Committee and work out the details?"

Sport was squirming in the background—Popsy could feel him writhing—but he kept his eyes on the fat red face. It was a good deputy sheriff's face, an after-dinner face, an arteriosclerosis face, a face on the other side of the streaked used-car window, and the nose came straight down from the forehead with only a slight lump of cartilage, a face developed before there were nose-guards on football helmets. He remembered Gut kicking the hell out of him in a losing season when he was flunking out of high school and busy half the night doing his ignorant best to get what's-her-name knocked up and thinking of joining the Marines. It had been a scientific beating, the kind any good police sergeant can give if he feels like it or if he knows the guy against the wall has a good lawyer. The big offense was having mocked Gut in front of other people, when it was a waste of prestige to get into a slanging match with a kid, and although Popsy had quit school instead of flunking, hadn't quite knocked her up, and had decided against joining the Marines, it had been a bad year for everybody around him, including him. He got a good whiff of the Depression right up his nose then, and if he hadn't found out he could sing and copy other people's gags, it would have been cold winters from then on.

He said, "You running a clean game here, Your Honor?"

"I don't know what you mean."

"I mean who's the man? Where do I put the fix in?"

Haggis settled deeper in his chair and twiddled his fingers on the arms. "I don't know what you're talking about."

"Where's the game?"

"I'm afraid you'll have to go outside the city to find any of that."

"Want to bet?"

"I'm not a gambling man, Popsy. What about the parade tomorrow?"

His brains felt like the eggs on the plate: not quite warm, floating on a watery residue, all the grooves scrambled. "I want to call a girl, Your Honor."

"Lots of girls in the phone book. I thought that was your specialty."

"I mean a girl. Give me a number."

"Afraid I can't do that."

"Would you like me to show you one in five minutes?" Popsy said.

"No, I wouldn't. I suppose you're trying to tell me something by all this?"

Popsy toyed with his tomato juice: it would be good for him, it was probably his own blood coming back as a special refund. But his hand was too jittery. "I'm telling you I don't have a very high opinion of cities. Are you sure this city wants to show its high opinion of me?"

Somebody started rapping on the door, and Sport went to take care of it. Haggis said, "Well, we'll give it a try. Just don't invite anybody to any imaginary parties between now and tomorrow morning. If we're going to ride in the same car, I don't want any stink bombs in with us."

122

Popsy mulled it for a minute longer. He knew he wasn't really thinking, knew that something besides the fairly reliable part of his brains was telling him to go ahead and do it, but he said, "Okay, but Kitch Steinway has to agree. Nobody gets sued or bothered for anything that's happened so far."

"Right. Make a note, Miss Chambers."

"And just the parade, just the big beautiful smile, no banquets, no singing, no press conference, no big deal at the stadium while thousands yawn and your little niece Gertie hands me a bouquet."

"Check. Got that, Miss Chambers?"

"Yes, sir."

Popsy said, "Miss Chambers, how do you feel?"

She looked at him blankly. "Just fine, Mr. Meadows."

"Not a little bit sick? A little indisposed?"

She hesitated, glancing at Haggis. "Well, now that you mention it—"

"Aren't you a civil servant?"

"Yes."

Haggis said, "Now hold on here. What's all this?" He struggled up out of his chair, having to uncross his ankles and lever with both arms.

"It's a new fiscal year," Popsy said. "Don't you have some sick leave left?"

Sport came back from the midget vestibule, looking mad. "There's somebody named Crackerjack or something who says he's not going to stand for this indignity."

Haggis said, "I'll be right there. Come on, Miss Chambers. And where do I find Mr. Steinway?"

"I'll show you," Sport said.

In a brisk business-like voice, Miss Chambers said, "I don't feel very well, Mr. Haggis. May I have the rest of the day off?"

"No." Haggis got hold of her elbow, his face darkening.

Popsy said, "I don't want to see any Arrangements Committee. Just fix it with Kitch." He leaned back in his chair with the tomato juice, smiling. "Goodbye, everybody. Everybody." He said the last so Sport would know, and although the voices went on for a little while, he didn't answer them. He closed his eyes till he heard the door shut, then held his nose and drank the juice. He felt he needed all the blood he could find, even if it was just getting some of his own back.

Adjusting the pillows behind his back for the tenth time, he scattered the newspapers, shut off the TV with the remote-control button just before the announcer opened his mouth to let out the late afternoon news, took a swallow of the Tom Collins on the bedstand, and listened hard. He couldn't hear anybody in the room beyond the connecting door, nothing from the room behind his back, nothing much from the street—only the high uneven whine of the air-conditioner and the same kind of whine inside his head like an echo. And it was bad because if it got turned up, even slightly, he wouldn't be able to keep close track of the noises around him, and you could never tell when it might be crucially important to tell the difference between an honest footstep and a stealthy one, between floorboards creaking with old age and floorboards giving under the weight of some creep, between the giggle of a chambermaid being pinched by a bellhop and the snicker of some

124

hairy mouth-breathing one-woman fan club who'd come to pay her dues.

Too many people had already come straggling in to see him: their cigarette butts were overflowing the ashtrays, their behinds had wrinkled the bedspread all the way around, three of them—whose names he'd forgotten—had told him the same joke. And they'd all wanted to chatter about the party, who'd said and done what, where so-and-so had been when such-and-such happened, what X had said to the manager when Y was doing something to Z, like high-school kids after a dance trying to figure out whether something memorable involving them had actually taken place. And five other people—two of whose names he got right—had come whisking in past Sport to tell him, one at a time, that another party had started farther down the hall, and two of the girls had already been high again and had garbled their lines like the bit players in the old jokes trying to say, "Hark, I hear a pistol shot!" or "Get your bus here for the Hotel Astor."

He felt dreadful. It was a womanish sort of word, and he tried to remember which of his flames had used it the most, and couldn't. But something bad was going to happen either inside or around him or both. He couldn't hear it coming or smell it or see it, but when the connecting door opened softly and slowly, he knew it was on its way and his eyes and his scrotum shrank at the same time, even before Mary-Mary stuck her head around the edge and smiled at him.

She said, "Hi, there."

"I told Sport I—" He cut himself off, unable to think of a polite way out of the sentence.

125

"I know you're tired." She shut the door quietly behind her. "Who'd know it better than me?"

She was wearing some kind of expensive yellow muumuu that suggested the extent of her figure without spilling it. No dress ever designed could hide *all* the facts about some-one like her, and Popsy considered praying.

She said, "I didn't know you had it in you."

"I don't." He'd known her for years. They'd done variety on the same bill, they'd toured USO, he'd been on her TV show three times, she'd given him a lot of laughs including dirty ones, but never in his weakest bleariest stupidest moments had he ever considered getting into bed with her—as far as he knew, nobody had tried it for years—and he must be out of his mind. He put one hand on top of his mind and gave it a nervous pat, like a man trying to get in good with a horse. He said, "What you have to hear right away, old pal, is I honest-to-God don't remember anything about last night." He made a circular gesture around his temple. "I need a new needle or some-thing."

He watched her face go slowly to pieces: first the heav-ily made-up dark-red wide mouth went down in the corners, then the craggy creased cheeks rose up against her lower eyelids, and the end of her nose turned pink under its powder. She said, "Before I could even—" She fished some Kleenex out of her small purse and got it ready.

He said, "Look, between old friends, I didn't want you to say anything you'd regret. You dig, Mary-Mary?" The trouble was she looked funny as hell, even now. She was too good at looking funny. "I think I'm sick, see?"

She said, "Oh, for Christ's sake."

He could see *that* wasn't going to cut any mustard, so he said hopefully, "Besides, nothing really happened anyway, did it?"

She slumped down at the foot of the bed with her back to him and began sobbing. For a moment, he just watched. She was too far away to pat, except with his foot, and that probably wouldn't help much. He remembered trying it once with somebody else and being accused of trying to kick her out of bed. He said, "Come on, don't go boo-hoo on your muumuu." But instead of laughing, she sobbed a little louder.

The telephone on the bedstand rang, and he answered it automatically without stopping to remember whether Sport or the switchboard operator was catching the foul balls for him today, and Belle Sanders said, "Hello, it's me."

"Hang on a minute." He jammed the receiver against his bathrobe. "For godsake, Mary-Mary, go take a cold shower or something. Please. I didn't mean to hurt your feelings." Already he could feel the sweat standing out on his forehead as he tried to figure out what to say to Belle. What had he been thinking about yesterday? And the day before?

Mary-Mary said, "What about our baby?"

Quickly into the phone he said, "Just another second, please." Then he capped it again. "Our what?"

"You said—" Mary-Mary was having trouble getting anything out between deep quiet sobs. "You said—"

"Act your age, Mary-Mary. You're older than *I* am." Then into the phone, "I tried to call you, but I—"

Belle said, "Yes, I tried to call you too. Who's with you?"

"Oh, it's just Mary-Mary having some kind of a—"

"*Just* Mary-Mary!" Half turning, Mary-Mary gave him a swampy look out of a mixture of mascara and eye shadow that extended all the way over the bridge of her nose like a raccoon mask.

He didn't feel like trying to get to the extension in the other room: he probably couldn't keep the door shut against somebody built like Mary-Mary anyway, so over the phone he said, "She's rehearsing a new routine. Lost-and-Found Department."

Belle said, "I saw you on the news."

"Oh, that. Yeah." He fished around for an answer, but the bottom of his mind felt like an empty washbowl.

Belle said, "Then I read the afternoon paper. I'm glad you didn't come all this way just to see me."

He considered the colorlessness of her voice. "Well, I would have if you'd asked."

"Doesn't make much difference now, does it? You're here."

Mary-Mary said, "You said we could have a little baby that looked just like me, only a boy." Her mouth turned down again and she started another series of sobs.

Belle said, "What was that?"

"Nothing." Mary-Mary's weight was making the mattress tilt up at his end like a hospital bed, and he felt ready for one. "I don't know exactly what's happening, Belle. Maybe you'd better come on over."

"I don't feel like it. I'm tired of reporters. Oh, happy birthday, a day late. I didn't get you anything."

"Thanks. Then meet me some place tonight. I'll make it alone." He tried to analyze his feelings, to trace the emotions he thought he'd set aside for Belle, but it was all like a tangle coming out of an old-fashioned wire-recorder gone haywire. "There's a place called The Finger with a back door. Say ten o'clock."

"Not me. This is my hometown too."

She was making him mad, but he tried not to let it into his voice. "Okay, kitten. It's up to you. But I had a nice weird proposition for you."

"I'll bet you did. They've all been pretty weird."

Mary-Mary said, "Don't you ever get tired of propositioning people? They ought to call you Propsy."

He ignored her, and Belle said, "I had a bad case of you, but I think I'm over it. It wouldn't have worked. There's too much difference."

She sounded as if she'd interrupted her own last sentence, and he waited a few blank seconds before saying, "What difference?"

Sounding a little flustered, Belle said, "We just think differently, that's all. And you have to admit there's a pretty big spread. I don't mind you banging around so much, I mean nightclubs are a way of life, but all that stuff about having lots of babies—I'm just not *ready*."

He sat up too fast, and all the blood rushed to the back of his skull. "What?" He steadied himself, feeling like an astronaut making reentry. "What babies? Who wants babies?"

Mary-Mary said, "*I* do."

He capped the phone. "Shut up."

Belle was saying, "If you want to retire and take it easy, that's fine, you probably ought to, but I'm just getting started, and an actress can't keep taking nine months off to drop a litter."

129

"You can't tell me to shut up, you fat has-been," Mary-Mary said.

Capping the phone, he said, "I didn't mean shut up, I meant—"

"Shut up!" She struggled to get one of her shoes off, then wagged it at him. Her eye makeup was all the way down her cheeks now, and she looked like a wash drawing of herself.

Belle was saying, "I'm just not the type. If you need somebody to take care of you, that's not my kind of problem."

"Who said anything about— My God, I never told you anything like that. You must be out of your head. I'm raring to go, I'm as good as I ever was, and if you don't believe it, just come over here for a little while. I don't know where you heard—" He got up on his knees, ready to go left or right because Mary-Mary had to come around one side of the bed or the other. "If I said something when I was loaded, I must've been clowning."

"I'll show you some clowning," Mary-Mary said.

He held the receiver against his bathrobe and said, "Act your age, damn it."

Mary-Mary's voice went up to a roar. "I'm *your* age, *your* age. Take a good look."

He listened to the phone again and caught Belle in the middle of a sentence. "—to face the facts. It's okay to pretend for an interview or something, but when you're right up against it—"

Richie came through the connecting door, wearing an ascot, a dark-blue blazer, gray-flannel slacks, and a high-

130

ball. He said, "What's the game, what's the limit, who's the house, is there an empty chair?"

Mary-Mary said, "You're the goddamn limit if you ask me."

Hurriedly over the phone Popsy said, "I'll show you what you're up against. Let's get it straight: ten o'clock, The Finger, or else. I mean I'll figure out something for the parade, just for you."

Belle's voice sounded tired again. "Threats. Okay, tell me what threats have to do with love."

"I don't know." He tried to think. "I don't know."

Richie said, "Whoever strikes the first blow has lost the argument. Didn't you know that, Mary-Mary?"

She threw the shoe at Richie, missing but making him spill more than half his drink on the carpet. He retrieved the shoe before she could come hobbling after it.

Holding his hand over one ear to concentrate, Popsy used the most earnest voice he could muster over the phone. "Meet me. If I make a mistake, you can insult me in public. Do you think I came this far just to be in a parade?"

She said, "Okay, but don't expect anything. And tell Mary-Mary I don't blame her."

He tried to hang up first but heard the click before he could get the receiver into the cradle on the bed.

Mary-Mary started toward the hall-door, then went off balance and had to lean against the wall. Richie brought her shoe, knelt, and tried to get it onto her foot. She kicked at it, then at him.

Richie scrambled backwards and stood up. "Come on, laugh it off. So it's not a glass slipper, so what?"

Going across the bed on his knees, Popsy sat on the far side, feeling tired, waiting. He hollered, "Sport!"

Mary-Mary said, "I don't hate men, I just hate their guts."

"So do I hate my guts." Popsy rubbed his aching stomach, then hollered, "Sport!"

"Take a man apart, and what've you got?" Mary-Mary said.

Richie put his nose into his highball. "Don't tell me."

She raised her voice. "A couple of hamhocks, a rump roast, spare ribs, enough giblets to last the cat a few days, enough fuzz to stuff a doll's pillow, a skull that wouldn't even make a good bird-feeder. You think just because you've got pants on, you can boss everybody around?"

Richie said, "Popsy doesn't have any pants on."

She said, "Look at the both of you. I've lost better eyes than that playing marbles. Want to Indian wrestle? The trouble with most little turkey cocks doing the struts all over the barnyard, they don't even know there's a war on. They think they've got the upper hand when all they've got is bad eyesight."

Popsy knew what she'd be looking like by this time, so he didn't look. He held his bathrobe shut and tried to remember what he was doing here. "Sport!"

She said, "Okay, now, straighten up for short-arm inspection. Don't worry, you can have it back when I'm through with it."

He heard her struggling with Richie, but he didn't turn to watch.

She said, "Come on, I'll make a cigarette lighter out of it."

Richie said, "Hey!"

Giving it the timbre of a last note, fortissimo, Popsy hollered, "Sport!"

She said, "I'll give you a free idea, Richie. Put up your breath in spray cans and sell it to the riot squad."

Richie said something, but the sounds of their shuffling were farther away, and the hall door banged open while she was saying something back, then Richie laughed and grunted from the hallway. He needed sleep badly: everything was hurting everywhere, but how could he sleep with people pouring through?

Sport said, "You want me?"

His voice sounded thick, and when Popsy turned to focus on him standing in the doorway to the hall, he saw the drink and the half-closed eyes and the wide stance, and he felt fed up. "People have been coming through here like it's the way to the can. Lock up and keep them out, please, what am I paying you for?"

"How should I know?"

"You're loaded."

"You're damn right I'm loaded," Sport said.

"Okay, you're fired."

"You can't fire me. You don't even know where the trigger is. You couldn't find the trigger if you had a map and a week to hunt."

He looked at the small erect wobbly man in the neat blue suit and said, "Just go away, Sport."

Sport went away, leaving the door wide open, and for a moment Popsy tried to gather the strength to get up and shut it, but the mattress gave too much under his hands. It was like being in muck or quicksand, and then a thirtyish woman in a silk-print dress with her coppery hair all piled up on top of her head came through shyly and nervously, closing the door behind her.

She fidgeted near the bathroom door, gave a brief bright smile, looked all around, and said, "I'm not sure I should even be here."

Getting a cigarette out of the bedstand drawer, he stuck it into his mouth unlit and quit looking at her. "You and me both."

After a pause she said, "I ought to say no. I feel awful risky coming up here like this."

"If you want to say no, go ahead and say it." He got up and walked past her into the bathroom and took three yellow Nembutal capsules.

"It's like a scene from a movie. You being so famous."

He came out and looked around the room and didn't want any part of it. He glanced her up and down and felt the same way. "What kind of work do you do?"

"You mean besides the restaurant? Well, hostess is the best so far. I wouldn't want to go back and do any of the other things. I had to work my way up from waitress, you know."

"Well, it's been nice talking to you." He felt as if he'd been killed earlier in the day and, because of the weather, was just now starting to turn cold. That was it, he'd been killed early in the morning, and nobody had figured it out yet.

She touched her hair, lifting both arms so that her breasts rose under her tight dress. "I can't believe it, me talking to you. I'm very flattered you took an interest."

"I'm the soul of generosity."

"I always heard you were the soul of generosity. There was that article in *Screen Gems*. And when you called me up, I—"

"*I* called you?"

"—I could hardly believe it. I didn't think you'd noticed me, but then they say smart people notice everything."

She was smiling awkwardly as though adjusting her upper lip to show the right extent of tooth, and he took her by one elbow, shook it, and steered her toward the hall door. "I'm not feeling very well, so I hope you don't mind."

"Oh, I'm very sorry."

"We'll do it some other time." He opened the door and Richie was leaning against the jamb like a salesman.

She said, "Do what?"

Richie took her hand and pulled her past him gently. "Never mind, lady, don't wreck the suspense. Tune in again tomorrow."

She said, "Should I save you a good table?"

"You do that." Popsy tried to get the door shut, but Richie had his foot in it, then his whole leg, and then he was sliding inside and latching it behind him. "Pop, you really go through them in a hurry. I had to give Mary-Mary a pill, and now this one—"

After bolting the connecting door, Popsy shoved the dresser in front of it. "Don't talk to me about dames. I've had it."

"Don't be bitter, don't be a quitter. Up, up, and play the game."

"I've played the game every way there is to play it. Some game."

Richie gestured with a fresh highball. "The sport of kings. I'll admit you've had some pretty weird types."

"Get out of here, I'm tired. And what do you mean, weird types? I've had the pick of the crop. Name a prince, name a duke, name a goddamn count that got somebody before I did." He waited while Richie thought. "Name a bullfighter. Name a senator. Name a baseball player."

Richie let himself be nudged toward the hall door. "Popsy, you've got a very ancient problem, though: what to do with used dames. Your closets aren't big enough, and if you leave them in the basement, they just get mildewed, and the garbagemen won't take them unless they're in proper containers, which most of them aren't. I don't know, maybe you ought to board them out some place. Start a dame farm. You'd have to keep the little ones separate from the big ones or they'd hurt each other. Separate cages."

"You think you're kidding?" He reached around and got the door half open.

While he squeezed out backwards, Richie said, "Then if the kings and all the other second-rate talents wanted to shop for a used dame, they'd know where to go."

"You know where you can go too." He tried to smile.

Through the last half-inch slit of the door Richie said, "There's another good one starting down the hall. You know, this isn't a bad town."

He shut the door on the middle of his own groan, made sure it was locked, and managed to get out of his bathrobe before he dropped himself on the bed. He lay there spread-eagled like a sky diver without a chute and started the long fall, the long erratic trajectory into sleep with his mouth wide open, either singing or screaming. No, he'd been killed earlier, that was right, and he was going to look like this till the last makeup man came and sewed his big mouth shut.

Keep flying, Baby, they'll write your name in smoke.
Keep dealing, Baby, and you'll go for broke.
The last one's down and dirty like the end of a joke.

Chapter seven

Leaning on the air-conditioner, he glanced at the parade forming in the street below, a huge muddle of band uniforms and floats, official cars and fire trucks, gangs of kids dressed up as something or other, horses and motorcycles and girls in bathing suits. Then swallowing half a warm highball, he tried for the tenth time to get Sport or Kitch on the phone but nobody was answering, which was typical of the kind of support you could expect when it came right down to the wire. He hadn't fooled around waiting till before breakfast to have his before-breakfast drink but had got up a couple of times in the night in order to get a good start on what had to be a good big day, a red-letter illuminated special with a concealed electric organ doing stings every couple of minutes. But now when it was time for a legitimate before-breakfast drink, there was nobody around to take up the slack, nobody to tell him to change his necktie and eat his cereal and comb his hair better over the thin spots, and what was the use of paying stooges if they weren't going to stooge? All he had was Haggis on the phone about every ten minutes and a corridor with nothing in it except some bottles—he checked it again to make sure, and now there were two cops in it, smiling at him—and he would have to get up his steam all by himself, without help of parent or teacher, just some more bourbon.

He considered hunting for Richie, but Richie was the only guy he knew who drank more than he did, and he didn't feel like starting a contest. Instead, he crossed the hall, knocked, then used the passkey on Sport's room. Nobody, no suitcases, and the bed was made.

"Something we can do for you, Mr. Meadows?" one of the cops said. "It's a couple minutes yet."

"No." If Sport had run out on him—

The second cop said, "My kid's got all your records."

"That so? I wondered where they all went." If they liked it once, they'd love it twice.

The cops chuckled and nudged each other, and he felt better. But then some of the real questions started hitting him as he stood uncertainly in his own doorway—What am I doing here? What's the percentage? What am I? What am I waiting for?—and while they watched, he finished his drink and went back inside for another, leaving the door open, feeling the ache start below the lower left edge of his ribs where his telephone gland was located. He needed to call somebody, but he couldn't think of any dialogue. He was underrehearsed. That was what was wrong. The part of his mind that was in charge hadn't given him enough time with the script, had only flashed his sides at him a few times, and let it go at that. And now he was supposed to go on.

Kitch came through the doorway, hitting one side of it and wandering catty-cornered over behind the sofa before he stopped himself and held on. Popsy had never seen him drunk before, and it was amazing—like seeing a preacher loaded in the pulpit or a bank manager living it up behind the loan desk. Then one of the girls from the party—a short young one with a lot of apparatus, wearing a salmon-colored pants suit with all the buttons off the front of the jacket—came through the door after Kitch and got hold of his arm as if she'd lost him in a crowd for a few seconds.

The first cop stuck his head in. "Okay?"

"Yeah, sure," Popsy said.

"Half a minute."

"Sure." Popsy checked himself in the wall mirror, and he was all right from a distance, and then he checked Kitch who still had a blue ribbon taped to the lapel of his char-coal-gray silk suitcoat, though his brown slacks belonged to somebody broader and taller.

The girl gave Kitch a little squeeze, and he steadied himself with his feet splayed out like a ballet dancer who was about to do something hard, but then he didn't do anything. He put the flat of one hand on his bald spot and seemed to press down. He said, "Why should you have it all?"

"Haggis says you okayed everything, right?"

Kitch sounded like some kid trying to do an imitation of The Shadow with a wool sock over the mike. "Am I some kind of example maybe? Was anybody ever meant to look like this?"

The girl said, "Go on, you're cute."

140

Kitch said, "D'you *learn* anything looking at me? Probably makes you feel better. I'm a lesson." His speech wasn't exactly slurred, but he wasn't making all the stops either.

The second cop said, "All set, Mr. Meadows?"

Popsy started herding Kitch and the girl toward the door, and Kitch went hand-over-hand along the wall like a rock-climber doing a tough traverse, till the girl got hold of him again. Kitch said, "God wouldn't create *me* just to make *you* a little happier, would he?"

"Didn't I give you a nice ribbon?" Popsy got the door shut behind them, then gave each of the cops a twenty before he could forget. "Better get some sleep, Kitch. It's tomorrow already."

The cops led the way to the elevator, and Kitch tried to keep up for a while, finally sagging into a doorway where he leaned. The girl jiggled him and began talking into his ear.

Suddenly speaking louder, Kitch said, "That's right, this little girl's going into the business like the rest of us. Now, I don't mind a bit part. I don't even mind a walk-on. But just to be some kind of prop!"

One of the cops punched the button, and Popsy looked back. "What's the matter with you? Isn't ten percent enough?"

Kitch said, "I won't *want* to make you feel good. Look at you, your clothes fit. Don't look at me, mine don't fit, and I don't want you to feel good."

Over the twenty intervening feet, Popsy said half-seriously, "I'm going to get a *secret* agent, Kitch. Somebody I don't notice, who's always some place else or pretends he doesn't know me."

"All right, I don't know you," Kitch said.

141

"Somebody who winds up getting shot at dawn."

"I was half shot at dawn." The girl pulled him off balance, but he straightened up again.

The elevator doors opened, the cops went inside, and Popsy said, "With a last fag in his mouth."

"Well, I didn't go that far."

Popsy went into the elevator and took deep breaths to keep his energy up. It wasn't easy to find straight-men, and Sport and Kitch were getting out of hand; you had to be careful of short guys because they were always trying to make another inch somehow, especially if they'd had a couple. It was better to have big ones like Fred, his body-guard, who was the size of the two cops put together and who could seldom get his ambition to crawl past mashed potatoes and gravy. But the world was filling up with wise-guys, mostly short and fast, as if somebody'd started a Wise-Guy School of Dramatic Arts and was turning them out and setting them loose all over the country.

The first cop said, "Something wrong, Mr. Meadows?"

"Breathing exercises." He went on taking deep breaths, but every time he let them out of his mouth, he could tell there was nothing between his lungs and his tongue, no voice box at all, and for godsake, what could he do—buy a midget electronic sonovox like somebody whose pipes had been reamed out by cancer?

Then the doors slid open, and there was Haggis in a pale summer suit he'd already sweated through and a big gang of what the newspapers, when they were feeling friendly and it wasn't going to cost them anything and the reporters didn't feel like writing out all the names, call *dignitaries*, each with his homemade wife and a couple of cronies.

They were strung out in a ragged reception line two-thirds of the way around the lobby, and Popsy gave them a modest kind of one-handed salute when their voices went up into a babble that wasn't quite a cheer but consisted mostly of everybody trying to tell everybody else what he looked like and when they'd seen him last.

While the happy friendly-sounding chatter was still going on, Haggis started to introduce him along the line, giving office titles for some and getting the wives' names wrong half the time, and Popsy went along with the gag, letting people remind him of imaginary times they'd all gotten together with so-and-so over at blank's house and weren't those the days and also letting some of the dumplings have a little smack on the cheek because it was late morning and there was nothing else to do and they bought records sometimes. The flashguns were popping all over the place, and he shook the hand of the bald Water Commissioner and got into a momentary grip-contest with the City Treasurer and tried not to listen to the endless bromides coming out of Haggis, as though off an endless-belt tape-recording: he never did the same one twice in a row but he'd repeated his whole bag three times before they were halfway through.

It was hard to direct a crowd scene, and whoever had put this one together hadn't paid enough attention to casting: the women all looked like cousins who did each other's laundry and fixed each other's hair and traded dresses once a week in rotation, and after the first big build-up of excited voices, the noise went down to a fairly level murmur, as though they were embarrassed now over having gotten geared up about seeing the aging hometown wonderboy in the excess flesh, the idol of the airlanes and the airlines, the popular nightclub sparring partner of the greatest and the most minute, the King of 78's and the Marquis, maybe, of 33⅓'s, the maker and unmaker of starlets, because after all there were lots of rich men in the world and lots of fast talkers and lots who could carry a tune.

One of the home-churned salt-free wives said, "Oh, you've been a bad boy. You've been touching up your photos."

He didn't reply to anybody directly, ignoring both needles and bouquets and letting Haggis fill in the gaps like a loud linebacker. It wasn't that he couldn't think up his own dialogue or was afraid to start something, but he had a growing sense that this was going to be a very very demanding day, no matter what kind of schedule Kitch and Haggis had agreed on (if any), and he needed to ration himself—not just on the flask he could feel clamped between his left biceps and his heart, but in every way. It was going to be a thick day, and he was going to be in the thick of it, in the major shooting, because there was a whole lot still to be done.

Then finally near the front doorway he was meeting Mrs. Haggis, who didn't look local—or, if she was, had obviously been finished somewhere else—and he gave her a good kiss on the severe lips for the photographers, after which she tugged at her severe white suit and looked flustered, and Haggis said something funny enough to get a laugh out of the nearest Councilmen. She was in her middle forties and clearly was too much for Haggis to handle even with an assistant coach, and it pleased Popsy to see a complication like that. It looked like Haggis had gone East and married a little money, though maybe it was only as far East as St. Louis or Chicago, and now she had him in the pencil sharpener and was giving him a few turns every day.

A cluster of a half-dozen cops waited beyond the doorway on the sidewalk, and when Haggis gave them the high sign through the glass door, they joined hands and played a kind of shuffling ring-around-a-rosy till the mob had cleared a path to a black Chrysler Imperial open-topped parade car, both ends of which were out of sight behind gawkers.

Then, having said nothing but "Hi" and "Good to see you," Popsy let himself outdoors first and stopped between the first cops under the hotel canopy and spread both arms in the big salute like a bullfighter, letting Mr. and Mrs. the Honorable Ormond Haggis bump into him from behind and stall there, not even off the welcome mat yet, while he took the cream off the top of the earliest outside applause and cheering. The loyalists (*some*body's fans; if not his, then Richie's or the ones who owed Haggis something) had come to the hotel, and if there were others who felt more like throwing tomatoes, they'd picked a different place to wait: the applause had a pretty good measure of tie-score eek in it, the kind of noise a crowd makes when it sees something good enough to eat and can't quite have it.

He walked briskly then to the car without giving any signals backwards and stood up on the back seat and waved all around before sitting down in the middle of the folded top. There was a VIP station between the jump seats, complete with a chrome handle to steady yourself with for a long stand-up ride, but he didn't feel like standing. With his feet planted on the seat and his arms braced on each

145

side, he watched Haggis and his wife figure out where to sit: after a moment of whispering hesitation, Mrs. Haggis clambered through and sat primly on the proper seat next to Popsy's left foot, and Haggis stood up on the back seat and waved to a much calmer second wave of noise, then smiled down at Popsy as though expecting him to move over. But Popsy stayed put in the middle, and Haggis had to sit at an angle on the outer edge with his back turned halfway toward the curb.

One of the high-school bands had struck up a heart-breaking off-key version of something or other, the drums coming along loyally and steadily a sixteenth behind the beat, and from where he was sitting he could see the lead-off units of the parade being wedged into place ahead of them, shuffling out of a side street under the command of a bowlegged major-domo with a red face and a clipboard. A hard knot of autograph hounds came over the curb and through the cops and stretched their programs and bound books and scraps of package wrapping over the rear deck of the convertible, and he signed a few and then kept giving the rest to Haggis till the kids gave up in disgust. And a kind of joke band behind them—the players all wearing cornstalks and shucks—started whanging away at a hill-billy number he remembered recording in about the Year One. It was a fine clear day, not too hot, and he had a little drink out of the flask. Luckily he'd already swallowed before Haggis nudged him hard.

"You're not going to do that, are you?" Haggis said.

"Do what?" A couple of flashguns went off while he was getting the flask back into his pocket.

"Drink in public, for godsake."

"What do you think I am, a secret drinker?"

A thick-necked plainclothesman got behind the wheel and a paunchy sergeant got in beside him, and while the car pulled slowly away from the curb, Popsy took the flask out again and tapped Mrs. Haggis on the shoulder with it. She lurched away from it and sat in a deep crouch in the corner.

"I'll get you for this," Haggis said.

He checked Haggis's face, which had a big mechanical smile on it while they passed a swiveling TV camera, then offered him the flask before they got too far out of range. A set of flashguns went off together, making a single pop like a champagne cork, and Popsy said, "Cheese!"

Then there was altogether too much noise for anything but pantomime. A couple of clutches of Councilmen had been stuffed into two cars behind them, but the major-domo dealt a girls' drill team and the cornball band between the three official cars, and directly ahead of the Chrysler he put a two-horse rick full of unshucked corn on top of which sat what had to be Cornflower Princesses, eight or ten of them, dressed like cowgirls in cornflower blue.

Having to raise his voice above the racket, Haggis said, "If you pull anything else, all agreements are off. And move over."

Popsy stayed where he was and started waving left and right as they edged out into position at a steady crawl. The crowd along both curbs grew thicker as they turned the corner onto Main Street: jammed elbow to elbow and two or three deep, and as far as he could tell, nobody was mad at him. He studied individual faces again and again, for

147

seconds at a time, and they seemed actually glad to see him. A couple of women blew kisses.

A photographer joggling along beside the car said, "Scrunch down, Mayor, you're in the way."

Haggis said, "Go to hell."

And here they were, having a nice big American parade, an art form like nothing else on earth, which hadn't been born, hadn't even grown, but had just bumbled forward into existence by default because people were willing to stand still along streets, and you had to give them something to look at once they were there. The girls' drill team was drilling away behind them, their half-formed or already overgrown butts lollopping inside cream-colored shorts to a quick-step snare-drum pattern, their calf-high boots smacking the asphalt with mechanical anger and precision. Their drill officer, who looked like a retired WAC sergeant in horn-rimmed bifocals, had found thirty-five pieces of underage jailbait who wanted to work long hours learning the marching manual of arms—they were doing it now with white dummy rifles—and who figured they were learning something important or beautiful or useful when they managed to stay in line and guide right and keep in step. And there were probably a half-dozen other teams in back somewhere getting ready to stomp. He glanced over the stern deadpans in the team—girls getting ready to be somebody for a change—and they scared him.

Ahead, the Cornflower Princesses up on top of their heap of fodder were making those gracious little waggles of the gloved hand, left and right, the way the gym teacher or the lady from the Women's Club had shown them, and a couple of them were facing to the rear and turning on all

148

the juice they could in his direction, maybe under the impression he was going to judge their contest or else for the other reason: trying to focus the Miss Armory Screen Test and Weekend in Las Vegas Look on him. Haggis was apparently catching some of it too, because his mouth was hanging open a little and his Practiced Professional Public Pose was leaking at the seams.

Now they were crossing the intersection of First and Main, where he'd had his first auto accident, where he himself had once stood to watch the American Legion Drum and Bugle Corps bump into each other and louse up "The Stars and Stripes Forever" to a faretheewell, and once again the crowd noise went up to a Goose-Me-Again-Willy series of climaxes that made him feel his last record couldn't have been all bad, that the hacks and flacks staffing the trade papers and the distributors respectively had put their empty heads together and had done him in, just for something to do on a wet Wednesday. People were throwing things into the car, and Haggis got hit with a magazine and what seemed to be a plastic bag full of cookies, and Mrs. Haggis was brushing the small change out of her lap as though it were cat hairs, and he got beaned with a handful of peanuts.

Haggis got down off the back and stepped forward into the VIP slot, hanging onto the handle with one hand and giving a big wobbly Mussolini salute with the other, trying to upstage him. But there was more than one balcony in the world, so Popsy did the only proper thing and slid down onto the seat with Mrs. Haggis and put his arms around her to keep her from falling out. Most of the crowd and especially all the people in office windows above ground level

149

could see him fine, and he watched Haggis soaking up the increased applause and the laughter that probably sounded like cheering to a less experienced ear. He remembered how Haggis had somehow managed to be standing up facing the grandstands during most of a football game, particularly when the cheer leaders were doing anything upside down; it didn't matter whether the team was ahead or behind: Haggis would adjust his expression from grim determination to profound self-satisfaction in profile or full-face, and it didn't matter much of a damn what was happening behind his back on the field. His team could be coming off on stretchers with concussions or dislocated ankles, be dying of thirst, be one man short, be wig-wagging hopelessly for him to send in a play; but Haggis the Gut would be stalking back and forth in his old trench coat, scoring points in a different game.

So it was with great pleasure that Popsy took Mrs. Haggis by the cold heart and held on for a few minutes, through thick and thin, giving the Gut time enough to catch on without having to wait for the evening papers. Mrs. Haggis squirmed quite a bit and called him some names, and finally the Gut pulled his big head down out of the breeze and took a look backwards.

Popsy gave it time to register, then disentangled himself and slid up onto the edge of the backrest again, unscrewed the cap of his flask, and toasted everyone in sight. Haggis sat down on the regular back seat, looking thoughtful. He knocked one of Popsy's legs out of the way with the heel of his hand.

And Popsy let the sun shine on him as much as it wanted to. He gave the big smile and the big double wave, and one of the Princesses lobbed an ear of corn at him, but it bounced off the rear deck of the car and fell into the street, and he watched it give a whole file of the girls' drill team something to think about.

After a few more blocks the crowd thinned out, and the official cars did a right turn into a side street and then went down a parking garage ramp into the near-dark. Even before his car had stopped, Popsy was letting himself out onto the pavement, getting his feet under him in case the Gut decided to do a little punching.

But the Haggises got out the other side, acting serene as royalty, and Popsy found his hand being shaken for the second or third time by Councilmen, Bingo Commissioners, and other assorted thugs in charge of the city grab bag, not to mention their wives who weren't worth mentioning. And he felt relaxed and amiable enough to let himself be herded into a big elevator and whisked up to the top of whatever building they were in and let out in the jammed lobby of a banquet room whose tables were already two-thirds full of what looked like a mulligan stew of the Lions, Rotary, Elks, and Kiwanis with a smattering of Eagles thrown in to season the pot. And he felt so charged up, his fingers were crackling and he could spit lightning if he felt like it.

Richie came up to him, moaning about the parade and looking happy at the same time. He said, "I was behind a horse, and I don't use *behind* loosely—" waiting for the chuckles from the hangers-on, then trying to top it "—but the horse sure did."

One of the citizens laughed, and Popsy gave him a pat

on the head. But he didn't really have time for indulging other people in their fantasies of self-regard, and as long as there were any free doses of omnipotence lying around, he was going to take them for himself. And while he was standing there, waiting for them to clear the way to the speaker's table—a section on a foot-high dais where everybody could get a look at all distinguished visitors spilling their soup and getting lettuce stuck to their chins and trying to get the white meat to come out from under the bridge—he suddenly realized he had a womb, just like a woman, and that it was empty and aching to be made fertile and that it could only be done by some Superior Being. He touched his paunch with sudden self-consciousness. Was his belt holding it in too tightly? And if he ever really got pregnant, what would he give birth to? A beef roast? A wad of dough? A sackful of crushed records, all those old records rolled into one? Or himself, aged zero, calling for a new deal? Or a little bundle of horror, all teeth and blood and hair?

Richie said something else, and then Haggis was there, jawing away about his own censored version of the parade, and then they were all filing and weaving and shuffling up to the head table under the intense light from overhead. Popsy went right to the two mikes clamped to a lectern, but Haggis gave him a genteel unobtrusive nudge with his hip, then laid a big paw on his shoulder and sat him down in the next seat.

To fill in time while Haggis was calling everybody to attention, he had another pull at his flask, then listened while His Honor apologized for being late and for not being able to stay long enough to eat their scrumptious meal.

Haggis said, "We have to beat the parade to the stadium, you know, but I wanted you to meet and greet our own favorite son who insisted on stopping by to say hello. Now I know a lot of you went to school with Popsy Meadows or, like me, watched his career from a little bit ahead, or maybe some of you younger folks looked up to him in those bygone days as he started turning in those unusual directions toward fame and stardom and wealth. At any rate, at long last, I'm proud to be able to welcome him home where at least a part of him has always belonged. A man they used to call The Voice of America before a radio network stole the title, Popsy Meadows."

It wasn't particularly violent applause, somewhere between the Patty Cake and the Pizza Pat, but he stood up and took it and pulled out a little more of it with a wink and a smirk. Then he gave all the tables a serious look through the glare, shutting them up. He said, "As you can imagine, it's a crazy experience to be back here with Gut trying to call the signals again." Medium laughter. "This is a lousy town, and I never thought I'd get my nose near it again, but here I am." Nervous laughter. "Now, why am I here?" He paused as if for an answer, but not even a spoon rattled.

Feeling like an evangelist, he leaned further over the lectern. "I used to be able to forget about this place and some of the people in it. Whenever they popped up, I'd just cram the things I didn't want to think about back down in the bottom of the box. But the box got full." He could see a couple of reporters scribbling away, and he gave them a five-second break. "Look, I'm not a bad guy."

Haggis clapped, and a couple of people joined in, and

153

Richie said, "Hear-hear" and tapped his water glass with a knife.

Popsy said, "I did more benefits and charity shows last year than any three other guys in this business. I did free commercials for the spastics or something like that— fouled-up kids. I lent more money to old buddies than I spent. I didn't lie to any man, and I didn't hurt any woman physically."

Richie said, "How about the year before?"

"Shut up." He glanced around, making sure he had all available eyes and ears. "I'm a habitual: I get up almost every day, I go to sleep almost every day, I eat almost every day, I get drunk almost every day. And I'm losing my guts. I think of things to do—I mean I start thinking of writing my autobiography or doing comedy again—and I freeze up. I get like a fist. For hours. And it's like the fist belongs to somebody else. Ever try to open somebody else's fist? And then finally it opens up, and there's nothing in it. Just the palm of my hand."

They were listening like machines now, some with their mouths open, and the whole scene looked pretty good except he wasn't sure about the lighting. Maybe there was too much on him: he could feel the sweat collecting under his eyes. He said, "I don't happen to be married at the moment, so I have to supply my own advice for better or for worse, for richer or for poorer, in sickness and in health till death takes me apart. And my advice was 'Go back to the old hometown and see if something's rotten because that's where you started and maybe you got off on the wrong foot like half that drill team behind you today.'"

Three places away, Richie said, "If you're going to spill

everything, Popsy, you could sell it to *Life* or *Look* for a mint."

"Don't wake the baby." He turned to Haggis, who was looking pale and sitting on the far edge of his seat. "What's the least leaky charity in town? The one with the fewest pig-knuckles in it?"

"The Community Chest."

Nobody contradicted, so he took out his checkbook and started writing while he talked. "I'm not making a survey of my old high-school teachers. Most of them are probably dead like Haggis here. And I don't want to start probing public institutions like poolhalls, whorehouses, and police stations because they're the rocks on which our society is built or maybe stuck, and I don't want to blame the climate —though why anybody wants to live in a place that's either roasting or freezing like a side of beef is beyond me —and I don't want to blame the newspapers for teaching me false values because I've had a chance to teach them a few meanwhile, so we're even, and I don't want to blame any of my old buddies either. I see a couple of them here, looking a little fatter, a little balder, and a little unhappier than they used to." He finished the check, waved it back and forth, and handed it to Haggis. "Ten thousand simoleons to help keep the cold out of the Community Chest. When I think of the Community Chest, I think of it as flat and hairless and—"

Haggis, in an applause-milking tone, said, "Thank you, thank you." Everybody clapped, and Haggis came chiming in before they were finished. "And now we have to get back to the Cornflower Festival before—"

Keeping himself planted in front of the mikes, Popsy

said, "I'm not finished yet. I may look finished, but I'm not. And I'm not blaming my dear old mother's toilet training either, though I hope the municipal water supply has a little more kick behind it than it used to, and I'm not blaming my old man for kicking my butt religiously every Sunday, and I'm not blaming Lucille Winston for holding out on me for two and a half of my formative adolescent years— she had a better wristlock than the wrestling coach—till I started thinking of women as if they were some very very expensive punchboard."

Haggis was trying to nudge him aside, but he held his ground by gouging with his right elbow. "See that? He taught me that. No, I just want to emphasize: as long as I was going to pieces anyway, I might as well come back here where something put the pieces together in the first place—because, after all, the pieces might be useful to somebody. Gut here tells me if I'm a good boy he's apt to name a park after me, and I'd like that."

Reddening, Haggis said, "A recreation area. I said a recreation area."

"Well, just make sure there aren't too many lights in it at night so the high-school kids can practice freedom of religion. And now, without further ado, except to say hello to Georgie Bannister there at the fourth table who introduced most of my junior high class to the mysteries of self-abuse, I'll wish you all a very good afternoon, and leave you with the advice I learned at Gut's knee—he was best with his right knee: 'When in doubt, punt.' And believe me, I'm in doubt." He stepped back against the wall and had a pull at the flask in preparation for signing autographs, but nearly everyone from the head table was mov-

156

ing out. And Haggis and some equally large officeholder crooked their arms in his and started him toward the elevator.

He rode alone in the back of the Chrysler with his feet on one of the jump seats and his hands behind his neck, not caring whether there was anybody to wave to or not. He was mildly interested in the route they were all following and a little annoyed when he saw the now fast-moving procession of official cars was headed toward the baseball park where the local minor-league team had taken its dutiful season-long beatings for so many years. And if Kitch had been in on the arrangements, he was fired; and if he hadn't been, he was still fired. The plain and uniformed cops in the front seat were too far away to ask questions, unless he wanted to shout, and he had a feeling he was going to need his voice, what there was of it.

The remnants of what looked like a first-class traffic jam were being unraveled in the parking lot, and the last limping drill team was disappearing into the gateway under the center-field bleachers. The official cars had to slow down for a moment before following—to squeeze left onto the cinder track that rimmed the field. They all drove along the first-base line beside the single deck of uncovered grandstands and stopped near the dugout. The whole playing area was chock full of the parade lined up in straggling rows, the bands, the wagons, the crepe-paper covered floats in the shape of the state, in the shape of an ear of corn, one that looked like the shank half of a ham but was probably supposed to be something else; a gang of little girls, each dressed like a cornflower, and so on. And whoever played third base next would have his choice among a variety of reasonably sized horse apples when the first groundball came at him.

One of the nearby bands not in position yet was playing a waltz, which made marching a little tough for all those who didn't have three feet, and then Haggis led the way into a bunting-draped box near first base. Popsy got out and followed, and the official cars whisked off immediately the way they'd come.

Richie came out of a clump of Councilmen and took his arm. "How're you doing, pal? Feel okay?"

"Never better."

"I don't like the sound of *that*."

"What're you, a doctor?" Popsy filed into the box, watching Haggis maneuver a beefy plainclothes cop between them. Mrs. Haggis was nowhere in sight. The stands were about three-fourths full with more coming, and there was a TV camera in the broadcasting booth behind home plate and another about ten feet away, looking right at him with its red light on.

Richie said, "I've got two tickets on the 6 p.m. plane which eventually winds up in L.A. Want to go? Miss Armory and Warbucks have found each other, so I've got an extra."

"No thanks."

"Quit peeling the onion, Popsy. You wind up with nothing."

Some chamber of commerce type beyond Haggis started saying "Ladies and gentlemen" over a hand mike, and eventually an uneasy kind of half-quiet settled over the field and the grandstands.

Popsy said, "Everybody needs a good cry once in a while."

Leaning close, Richie said, "Mary-Mary and Alice took off already, sort of mad. It was a pretty good party. Let's cut out."

He knew Richie was trying to help, and he said "Thanks" genuinely, but shook his head at the same time.

The chamber of commerce type said, "Ladies and gentlemen, the massed bands under the direction of Sam Hart will now play our National Anthem, while a color guard consisting of veterans from the First, Second, Korean, and Vietnam wars will raise the colors, and our own favorite prodigal son, Popsy Meadows, under the direction of his first singing teacher, Miss Amelia Claybury Tucker, who has come out of retirement especially for this occasion, will lead us in the singing."

Popsy held the mike when it was shoved into his hand, and ten or twelve thousand people in the stands grunted and shuffled to their feet, some applauding, and old Miss Tucker, still with the same fogged-over glasses and a head of white hair that looked as if it had been made in a hurry out of hotel napkins, suddenly appeared outside the railing of the box, smiling at him expectantly, the way she had the first time he'd plowed through her arrangements of "The Riff Song" and "Stout-hearted Men" at the raucous school assembly. She was trying to keep track of the bandmaster over her shoulder, and when he gave the downbeat, she got hers in a quarter-note behind, and most of the bands came in even further behind than that, and at the last split second Popsy considered palming the mike off on Richie, who could at least croon the middle-register parts, but there was no telling, ever, what words Richie would remember—chunks of stag-party parodies, maybe, like the time he'd sung "The Lord's Prayer Cha-cha-cha" at Bishop Horton's birthday—so he put the mike up to his own face and began mouthing the words silently with exaggerated diction-class lip movements.

A number of people were singing nearby, using a kind of compromise beat among the conflicting band noises, and even Haggis was giving out with a gravel-throated baritone, so for a few bars nobody reacted. Then some T-shirted kid crouched over the P.A. system on the cinder track and fiddled with it till the loudspeakers started blasting, picking up the plainclothesman's toneless mumbling next door and Richie's halfhearted humming on the other side. The TV cameraman started knocking himself on the headphones, then made some hand signals to the mobile-unit truck near home plate.

He was already past "the bombs bursting in air," keeping a straight serious face, and the flag was sneaking up the flagpole in center field, and pretty soon it had to be time for him to find out what was eating him and find out whether he had to eat *it* in order to stay alive, because if he didn't have a voice, he didn't have a prayer. That extension of himself, that enlargement—it was like being in a thousand places at once, in as many places as there were ears listening, in as many shapes as there were minds being held in temporary suspense by the complex linear craft of song which he would never understand—that magnification of whatever was simultaneously powerful and worthwhile in his fattening heart. Had he simply treated it all too carelessly, treated the piece of physical luck in his throat and head like a bottomless bank account and wound up overdrawn?

He finished pantomiming "the ho-hum of the braaave" with his eyes blurred, then sat down and listened to the emcee trying to cover up with a line of gab. Richie was nudging him and looking ready to split with suppressed laughter. Then Haggis started windbagging about this and that over the hand mike, tapping it first with his fingernail, and the whole afternoon seemed to be melting.

Popsy half-listened to another phony résumé of his local career; then with a sudden inexplicable alertness, he started going over all the nearby faces, having to crane his neck to see around people, being especially careful to check people who appeared to be trying to keep their faces from him. He turned around in a low crouch and peered back through the higher rows.

Richie said, "Hang on, man, I think they're gonna have you throw out the first bottle of the season."

While Haggis went into his peroration, using the same kind of hard-shell Baptist rhythm he'd once tried to put on in a half-time spiel, Popsy stayed on the lookout for his old man and his mother because it was just the kind of This-Is-Your-Life trick a Corn King like Haggis would think up to round out a program. But they didn't seem to be anywhere in sight, and there were no good places for them to hide close by, unless they were stashed away out of sight around the corner in the dugout, waiting for the signal from the TV director.

And then suddenly Haggis was producing a genuine foot-and-a-half-long aluminum-painted plywood Key to the City with a blue ribbon on it—which some junior high-school shop teacher had probably jigsawed out in the middle of the night—and handing it over, accompanied by a series of trumpet flourishes from the nearest brass section that went haywire with triple-tonguing before it was half finished.

He took the key, but Haggis was keeping the mike in the far hand, not giving him a chance to say he was speechless or anything, and it was probably just as well. He waved the key over his head, and a lot of people seemed to applaud; then the emcee signaled and the various units of the parade started milling around the field, breaking up, most of them heading for empty seats. Somebody turned the sun up a few notches, and they all settled back to watch the first round of a cornhusking bee.

Richie said, "Still plenty of time to make that plane."

They stood side by side at washbowls in the home-team dressing room, while Popsy patted cold water on his sunburned forehead and nose. Their eyes met momentarily in the mirror, and they shook their heads simultaneously.

"I didn't think so," Richie said.

After he'd wiped his hands, Popsy took his Key to the City off the hook and started up the dim dank cement ramp behind Richie toward the dugout where a cop was guarding the door. He felt the old buzzing in his feet like an electric signal from the Boss, meaning get on the stick, get going, there isn't much time, time is money, you're running out of it, find out what the deal is, don't let the grass grow under your ass, fish or cut bait, move it, you can't make a nickel with your hand on a Bible, and if you can't find the action, be it. But the sense of urgency didn't come with

162

instructions, and when he clumped up the steps onto the field, he could only think of doing what they'd been doing.

Richie said, "Who should we give it to, for godsake? That fashion dame isn't going to be any help. Probably a butch, and they don't exactly consider the talent end of it."

"I don't care." Popsy glanced ahead of the Cornflower Princesses lining up on the portable wooden stage where all ten of them, one at a time, had recently finished butchering their carefully rehearsed song and/or dance routines. "The one with the broken nose who forgot the words is the daughter of an old buddy of mine, so let's give it to her. That'll teach him a lesson."

Richie shielded his eyes like an Indian scout. "Ordinarily I'd say give it to the one with the biggest boobs, you can't go wrong, but what the hell do they feed them around here, bran mash? And if I could only get them to turn around and drop those cowboy pants for a minute, I might be able to tell what I was looking at."

Popsy said, "How about a sack race?"

"That's it!" Richie signaled the other judge out of the box, a lanky dark-haired woman wearing a pink jockey cap and a pink minidress, and he started to tell her.

But she said, "If you don't mind, we'd better finish this because everybody's waiting and I personally consider it very rude."

"Didn't you ever hear of a call of nature?" Richie patted Popsy hard on the back. "My distinguished colleague has just had a great idea for another division in the contest: a sack race. Why don't we put beds at first, second, and third base, and each of us gets in one, and the girls all line up at home, and—"

The woman turned away, disgusted, and went striding toward the stage full of Princesses.

Richie said, "Is this really your hometown, Popsy?" He was beginning to look tired.

The buzzer went on again in his feet and stayed on. The Boss wanted something in a hurry, but he didn't know what it was. While Richie went over to the nearest Princess and started inspecting her teeth, Popsy turned and looked back at all the people in the grandstands. Haggis was box-hopping, the Councilmen and Commissioners were all seeping around doing missionary work, and the funny part of it was he didn't feel like drinking. A TV camera came rolling closer with its light on, and he stared back at its big eye, aimed the key at it, and gave it a half turn.

Amelia Claybury Tucker said, "You've come such a long way, and you have a nice pure tone, but I never thought you'd be a professional singer."

Something had gone wrong with her nervous system—was that what strokes did?—and she was nodding slightly all the time like a salesman trying to create a climate of agreement, and Popsy felt sorry for her. But the strain of being polite was making him sweat. He shuffled a little on the cinder track and looked around hopefully for Richie.

Miss Tucker said, "You never liked to practice, and that's a bad sign. And smoking!"

The emcee was awarding the last prizes for parade floats, including categories previously unknown to man, and Popsy was glad to be able to score a few points himself. "I don't smoke."

"I saw you smoking on television just last year."

"I quit. This year I tried doing everything right, but it isn't doing a hell of a lot of good."

She pulled back slightly. "Herman! Such language."

"Everybody calls me Popsy." And before she could answer or go into it at all, he added, "I've been having a little throat trouble, Miss Tucker. You know a good cure?"

"What is it, laryngitis?"

"No, I don't think so. I just—"

"Overstrain? You never *have* resonated properly. It's probably from antagonistic tension. Your inspiratory muscles aren't balancing your expiratory muscles. You're tensing your neck and relaxing your geniohyoglossus muscles. And I noticed you weren't getting anything like the proper volume with the National Anthem. Give yourself a good rest and a good spray of Vocalzone."

She went on talking, but the emcee came over and steered him firmly to the portable stage, now empty of all Princesses, and he let himself be led. If he was going to have to judge anything else, agree with anybody else, meet anybody, smile at anybody, wave at anybody, or listen to one more chunk of imaginary biography, he'd lose more than his voice: he'd lose the lunch he'd skipped.

Someone had parked a new white Ford pickup truck next to the stage, and after a few moments he penetrated the emcee's bafflegab far enough to understand it was being given to him "in case you ever decide to take up the simple life again." And then there was a string of apologies because it wasn't a Cadillac or a sports car, but Haggis, looking grim and wary, interrupted and nudged the emcee away from the mike and said, "We figured this was probably the only kind of vehicle good old Popsy might not own yet, courtesy of Tower Motors managed by Councilman Fred Baumgarten."

Haggis dangled the keys, luring him away from the mike, and Popsy took them and nodded his thanks around at the moderate applause. Then Haggis grappled him by the shoulder, led him up to the truck, and muttered, "You bastard, if I hadn't already put this in the papers, you wouldn't even get a kiddie car."

The truck had been doing something in the parade because they hadn't swept all the hay and crepe paper out of its bed; and when he leaned in the door, he saw it already had nearly three thousand miles on it, but what the hell. He stood on the running board, waved his Key to the City, then got in and turned on the ignition. The engine coughed, then caught on, and he drove forward onto the cinder track, carefully ran over a couple of sets of TV cables, and headed down the right-field line. He turned slowly onto the grass and honked the horn as steadily as a heart, aiming the pickup's nose at the open empty gate in dead center-field.

This is the right place, Baby. This is where it died.
There's the knocker, the rocker, the carcass and the
hide.
The door's wide open, Baby, come on inside.

Chapter eight

The sun had been wiped out without a trace behind a bank
of dark clouds and was either all the way down or almost
when he stopped the truck a half block short of his parents'
house-and-bar and got out. He gave himself another squirt
of Vocalzone, then tossed the atomizer onto the seat,
slammed the door, and had a good look at the dingy roofing
plant past the next corner where rolls of tar paper and
bundles of shingles were stacked in clumps and mounds; at
the opposite row of frame houses shaped like lunch buckets
where his boyhood friends and enemies and their scroungy
families had lived and were maybe still living; at the grass-
less strips between sidewalk and curb on both sides of the
street where the dirt was baked so hard by now, near the
end of summer, it couldn't be cracked with a pickax; at
the dust-covered dented new cars parked bumper to
bumper all the way through the neighborhood. He took a

whiff of the gritty air, then tried to breathe out more often than he breathed in, walking slowly toward the entrance.

His old man had changed the name again, and now it was the Crow Bar (after the Drift Inn and the Come On Inn and the Handle Bar and God knew what else) in flickering neon on a sign touting some off-brand of beer (a penny saved is a penny earned), but everything else looked the same, including the weatherbeaten gray paint which had also been slapped on the adjoining house. Maybe there had been a sale of old paint that looked old as soon as you put it on. He hesitated at the narrow steps leading up to the porch: he couldn't tell whether any lights were on behind the drawn shades, and he couldn't tell whether any lights were on in his head either which was feeling like a dime-store Halloween pumpkin with its candle on the blink. And as usual there was no graceful way to do anything he really wanted to do, only clumsy slew-footed worse-than-nothing ways that were going to leave him bad off by nightfall. This would be a bad night (how many in a row?) no matter what the Boss in the bottom of his mind decided. He took a deep breath as if to hit a big long finishing note, took the extra steps to the entrance of the bar, and went inside.

The early Saturday crowd wearing short-sleeved shirts and slacks instead of overalls was jamming the long row of barstools, but only a few couples were at the round Formica-covered tables. The tiny stage was empty, and the whole place was darker than he remembered—or else they hadn't changed to the night lights yet. Waiting near the door, he took automatic inventory of what was left from his own days here as swab-jockey, floor-waxer, bar-varnisher, glass-wiper, and occasional booze-thief: not much. Thirty years had made even his old man break down and replace a few fixtures. But the smell was the same; he'd kept the same air and the same kinds of people were reusing it, passing it around like a bucket-brigade version of mouth-to-mouth resuscitation.

He didn't know the tall, stoop-shouldered bartender, but the man knew him, and after one look he disappeared through the door to the storeroom which led to the inner door to the house, so Popsy stayed where he was, knowing he'd be announced. He checked the lineup on the jukebox beside him, and five of his records were on it, including a newish one, which meant he at least wasn't being boy-cotted.

Then his old man was in the storeroom doorway, shooing the bartender back to work, and he *looked* like an old man for a change—a cowlick of gray hair, his angular profile honed down even more sharply, his height seemingly cut by a couple of inches, the gray stubble of a two-day beard glistening on his cheeks.

Popsy walked toward him behind the long row of bar-stools, and it was like rattling a picket fence with a stick. Each man turned as he went by, catching on to what was happening, and called his name or made some kind of noise, and by the time he got to the end he felt like a leading chorus boy doing a trick number with a gang of top-hatted and dress-caned nancies.

But his old man got him over that feeling in a hurry. He said, "What the hell do *you* want?"

He didn't have to give it any thought. "I want my dinner."

His old man looked a little surprised but didn't get out of the doorway. "We've been watching you."

All the others had shut up now and were listening as hard as they could. Popsy said, "I left without my dinner, so I'll take it now."

"What a horse's ass on the TV."

He thought it over for two seconds, gauging the tone, then said, "I've got the Key to the City, Daddy-O."

"I wouldn't even give you the key to the back door."

The boys along the bar liked that one, and Popsy waited for them to shut up again. He said, "Okay, are you going to serve me in here or in the house? I think I'll have steak and potatoes." He took a folded twenty out of his pocket and began flicking it, watching his old man's eyes do what he knew they'd do.

After wavering for a moment, his old man said, "I'll see what we've got." He turned and started back through the storeroom.

Popsy ducked under the hinged section of bartop, peeled two twenties onto the floor between him and the bartender, and said, "See if the boys can drink that much without falling off." Then he followed his old man into the storeroom and through the next door and straight into the kitchen, and there was his mother at the stove, almost as broad as it was, wearing a faded print house dress whose hemline wobbled between calf and ankle. Her toes were inside her slippers, but her heels had crushed the backs down flat, and she wasn't wearing anything over her blue sponge-rubber curlers. She turned her expressionless moon-face toward him.

He groped for something to say. "Well, it's been a long time, hasn't it. I've been meaning to—"

170

His old man, speaking loudly, said, "He wants some dinner. Steak."

She seemed to think for a moment, then nodded. "That's all right."

It was too hot in the room, too humid, and the yellow curtains and the cracked yellow linoleum seemed to waver with heat mist. He said, "Good. Mind if I sit in the dining room?"

His old man had his hand out, and when Popsy put a twenty in it, he said, "Sure. Go ahead."

His mother watched the bill change hands, then said, "Our subscription to *TV Guide* ran out."

He peeled a twenty for her too, and she stuffed it into a pocket overflowing with Kleenex.

His old man said, "What do you need that for? If you want to know what's on television, turn it on and look. Why the hell do you need an expensive magazine to tell you what you're looking at?"

For a moment he thought of kissing his mother—it was what people did in movies and books—but he couldn't decide which part of her face to kiss. Her pale, swollen-looking cheeks seemed to have cold cream or something on them, and he didn't want to be seen rubbing his mouth afterward. And only for the briefest moment did he consider trying to shake hands with his old man: hands weren't for shaking, they were for working and maybe defending yourself, and if anybody wanted to shake your hand, you'd better watch what he was doing with the other one. Besides, his own hand was already shaking by itself.

His mother wrestled a large thin plastic-covered steak out of the freezing compartment of the refrigerator, got a potato out of the vegetable bin (brushing a handful of

171

inch-long sprouts out of its eyes), and set them on top of the stove. She said, "It gives the names of people on the programs."

"Didn't need any *TV Guide* today," his old man said. "All the fuss, you'd think nobody else ever learned how to sing a song."

Wandering to the dining-room door, Popsy held onto the jamb, neither in one room nor in the other. He could hear somebody moving around upstairs, but he didn't want to ask who it was. He said, "I realize there's bound to be a certain amount of bitterness, maybe you think I should've come around sooner or written more often, but we're all grown people, aren't we? Can't we start over from scratch?" His voice sounded tight and defensive, and he tried to smile some easiness into it. "Let's have a drink, Dad."

His old man sat down at the kitchen table, opened a newspaper, and flattened it full-length. As he squinted to read, he said, "Sure."

From the stove his mother said, "Mrs. Peterson's little boy was hit by a car, Mrs. Krustowski's nephew scalded himself with a pan full of fudge, and Mrs. Cutter's daughter's engaged."

Looking up indignantly, his old man said, "Do you mind? I haven't gotten that far yet."

"And Mrs. Kirkpatrick's boy went sailboating at night and turned up missing."

"How could he turn up if he's missing?" his old man said.

"Well, his boat turned up."

Popsy rubbed at the tension along his forehead and tried to remember how people made conversation. He felt he'd

172

never had a conversation with anybody before in his life. "Your friends sound careless with their kids."

"Plenty more where *they* came from," his old man said.

His mother was peeling the potato with a butcher knife, and he didn't want to watch. He glanced at the muddy-looking walls in both rooms: had they turned that color since he'd been gone? In his memory everything was harsher and more definite; objects had clearer edges, and there wasn't all this fuzz.

His old man said, "When I was working on the railroad, the gang foreman came over to me and said, 'Bud, can you lift a 250-pound keg of spikes?' I said, 'I don't know, I never tried.' So I got up and went over and the section hands were all watching, and I gave it a big heave—you know, you've got to use your knees, you've got to bend 'em and let 'em take the weight or you'll rupture yourself —and I'll be damned if I could move it an inch." He started reading the newspaper again.

After waiting a moment, Popsy said, "What's the point, Daddy-O?"

"What?"

"What's the point of your story?"

With a wry down-turn of his thin lips, his old man said, "If I hadn't tried, I'd never have known I couldn't do it. Now I know."

"And if you happen to run into a keg of spikes some place, you just leave it alone, right?"

"They've got machines to lift those things now," his old man said.

His mother said, "You want lima beans, Herman?"

"Anything's all right." He watched his old man for a few more seconds, then said, "How much is a drink?"

"You know the principles of business."

Popsy nodded. "I know: as much as the traffic can bear. Well, how much do you figure I'm good for?"

"A buck. No more, or you'd go out in the bar and get it."

He fished in his pocket and put a five on the table. "I don't have any change."

Leaning back without getting out of his chair, his old man groped in a cupboard below the sink and brought out a half-full pint of blended whiskey. "Now don't let it break your heart you don't have any change. If you want your change that bad, go on out to the cash register."

"Keep it."

"Giving things away." His old man shook his head. "Ever hear anything like that, Mother?"

She said, "Now, you two."

"Ten thousand dollars for the Community Chest."

Popsy said, "Can't we talk about something besides money? Look at me, I'm home. Do you believe it? I'm standing here." He looked down at where he was standing. "Why don't you have new linoleum? Business looks good. I send you checks all the time."

"Half the time." His old man slipped open the second button of his white shirt so he could scratch below his collarbone. "I thought you didn't want to talk about money."

His mother said, "The Smiths painted the inside of their house beige and cream and a pink powder room on the second floor, and it burned down the very next week."

"Let me tell you something," his old man said. "My first job, I worked door-to-door as a canvasser for a salesman,

174

and at the end of the first week when he owed me ten bucks plus fifty cents for the coffee I'd fetched, I couldn't find hide nor hair of him. That's the meaning of *thrift*."

Popsy let himself edge far enough back into the dining room to be out of the kitchen light. It smelled stale in both rooms, but it was as much upholstery-stale as food-stale. He couldn't see through the front windows, but it sounded as though somebody was revving up the peas in the rain machine and giving the thunder screen nervous little shakes. He said, "It's weird, isn't it. We're all grown up. We made it."

His old man said, "Made what?"

"I never thought we'd get this old."

His mother said, "Mrs. Albert's boy entered medical school last week, and he's going to get straight A's."

He came back to the edge of the kitchen. "Can I have a drink of water?"

"How about some milk?"

"Anything." He watched her wrench open the refrigerator like a stuck drawer. "If he just started, how does she know what his grades are?"

She said, "He tells his mother everything."

Somebody started cranking the wind machine outside the kitchen window but he couldn't see anything beyond the gauzy curtain, just a deepening grayness. He tried to remember what was in the back yard. Was there a back yard? His old man was prowling through the newspaper again, so just to make conversation he said, "I don't see how anybody can be a doctor."

"Don't worry," his old man said. "Not just anybody can be a doctor."

175

"That's what I said. I said I don't see—"

"I'd like to see *you* try it."

He took the tumbler full of milk from his mother and held onto it. "I don't want to be a doctor. I'm already something."

"What? What are you?"

"A millionaire, for instance."

"You don't have it, those women you married—they've got it. I read it in a magazine. Where's the cash?"

"Nobody keeps that kind of cash." He kept his voice down. "In case you haven't noticed, I'm at the top of my profession."

"Profession. What're you a professor of?"

"I'm a corporation. And I'm famous."

His old man put his left hand flat on the stock reports and his right hand flat on the want ads. "It costs a couple of bucks to form a corporation, and what the hell are you famous for? Playing grab-ass on TV?"

He took a sip of milk, then had to spit it quickly sideways toward the wastebasket, hitting the floor instead. It was warm and tasted like chemicals. He said, "My God, what's that supposed to be?"

"You clean that up now. Don't make your mother clean it up."

She said, "What's wrong, Herman?" She fanned herself absently with a spatula.

"It tastes terrible. I mean not even sour but foul."

"You watch your language," his old man said.

She said, "I don't know what it could be."

He set the glass on the table, picked up the pint, took a swallow into his mouth, rinsing his tongue and teeth. It

176

tasted worse, and he got to the sink in time to spit it down the drain.

His old man said, "You pay for it, you can do what you want with it."

Breathing in and out with his mouth open, he tried to make the taste go away, but it seemed to spread and come out of his ears: a mixture of ozone, sulphur, and cheap perfume. He said, "Somebody trying to poison me?"

His mother said, "You'd better have some baking soda."

He got away from the sink and into the dining-room doorway again, feeling jolted, with a sense of having had a near miss. Maybe his tongue was getting ready to run out on him too, maybe it would quit and go back down where it came from like his voice box, leaving nothing in the way but his teeth, which would then fall out.

"If you're so damn good," his old man said, "let's hear you hit high C."

He made a calming gesture with the flat of one hand. "Daddy-O, let's save everybody a lot of trouble. Don't ask me to hit anything."

"Barging in here after all these years." His old man scanned along a column of want ads with one forefinger.

His mother peeled most of the plastic off the steak and thumped it down in a large skillet, having to force the frozen edges down with the heel of the spatula. "Our own flesh and blood, remember." She smiled faintly over her shoulder.

His old man grunted, and Popsy turned halfway in the doorway, suddenly now getting it from all directions including upstairs and the basement and next door in the bar and from the neighbors and the front and back yards, from the living room and the closets, from the insides of furniture and mattresses and out of old drawers and the garage: the simultaneous attraction and repulsion of familiar objects, the rusty, dusty, worn out, greasy, cracked and streaked tangible objects of the house with their ancient history steeped into them like smoke into ham but without curing—wood, cloth, glass, iron, paper, china, leather, and plaster. And he felt like the Magnetic Man in the old movie with everything around him, light or heavy, being yanked in his direction whether he stood still, walked, or ran, everything coming closer on hair-thin wires, all aiming at one tremendous pig-pile with him on the bottom—books, rugs, lamps, porch swings, paint cans, shovels, trunks, stuffing, and photos that were going to put him to the test, yes or no, can you live under that heap or can't you?

He said, "I've been trying to do something."

"Why don't you sit down, Herman, it'll be ready in a minute, I don't know what got into your milk because it tastes all right to me," his mother said.

He went a little farther into the dining room, feeling the oak buffet and chairs shift with him and the big round table hesitate, getting ready to roll. Somebody nearly broke the crank on the wind machine, and the special-effects guys started pouring water off the edges of the eaves. Flashguns went off outside the dining-room and living-room windows, but whoever was working the thunder screen missed his cue because no sound followed. He waited a moment to be sure the levels were right so he wouldn't be drowned out, then he said, "You know, people want to find out where the action is, but *I make it*. That's the difference between you and me, Daddy-O. I don't have to find out where it is. I'm it."

His old man stuck his head through the doorway and turned on the dim old-fashioned salmon-colored bulbs in the brass chandelier. Two out of five were burned out, but the three good ones lit the sharp nose, the tufted gray eyebrows, the hard narrow pockets of flesh at the downturned corners of his mouth. He said, "Son, I've been meaning to tell you something for a long time. When a man and woman get properly married, it's like two little birds building a nest. After a while, the papa bird plants a tiny seed in the mama bird, and it gets bigger and bigger and bigger and—"

From the kitchen his mother said, "I don't like that kind of talk."

Picking the only dining-room chair with arms, Popsy sat in it and bellied himself up to the table. "What are you, seventy-five? Seventy-six? And you've never ridden a horse in your life. Never had a bottle of champagne, I'll bet, unless somebody left a couple of inches behind. Never given away anything worth more than ten bucks. Never been in water over your head. Never danced a step, not one step, not even by yourself. Never seen New York or London." He knew his voice was getting too loud, he wouldn't be able to keep it up, but the volume kept building by itself. "Never done anything in front of an audience, nothing. Never finished reading a book. And what the hell are you doing calling your wife 'mother'? Never found out what it's like to be somebody else because you never had enough nerve to pretend, so you don't even know your *own* goddamn lines."

"What a loudmouth," his old man said. "All the answers."

"All right, what's your next line?"

His old man shook his head. "No use arguing with a bigshot."

"That's not it!" He leaned back while his mother plopped a knife, fork, and spoon wrapped in a paper napkin onto the bare table in front of him. "You're supposed to say, 'What good did any of those ever do *you?*'"

"Say it your own self."

"Never went skiing, never saw a salmon except in a can, never stayed at a hotel that cost more than $3.50 a night, never seen an opera—" his voice was going up again, getting shrill, and he brought it back down a little while his mother plodded back to the kitchen. "Never given a party for more than four people, never bought your *mother* in there a dress." He felt winded, and how in God's name was he going to eat anything? Why had he even asked for anything? The peas were thumping against the screen of the rain machine, but whoever was doing the pickup didn't have the mike close enough to make it realistic. It sounded like it was raining next door instead.

His old man said, "Tell you what, Herman. Seeing's how you're over the hill and have went and blown all your dough on women and are getting too worn out to let the cameras get up close any more, maybe you better pick up some part-time work around here. They're starting to berry-pick down in Stark County. I could show you how, give you a head start on the others. What you want to do is don't pinch too hard. And if somebody in a long black fur coat tries to collect your bucket, make sure he's got shoes on first. Might be a bear."

180

Popsy looked at him through the rusty light. "Where do you pick up routines like that? Out at the bar? Down at the barber shop?"

His mother came back into the room, holding a plate in each hand and clucking. She said, "Not so loud." She put down a plate of toast, pointed at the ceiling, then set down a big blue dinner plate with a half-mashed potato, a lump of pale-green lima beans, and a dark-brown thin steak with a wobbly fatless edge.

He wouldn't have a chance of getting it into his stomach, not a chance, but he felt as if he'd proved something by having it brought to him.

Smiling, his old man said, "Want me to say grace?"

"Don't strain your water." He got his knife and fork out of their paper cocoon, then hesitated when he saw his mother and his old man get together at the far side of the table to watch. They were standing there, waiting for something to happen, and he didn't know how to make anything happen. He tried to cut the steak from three different angles, sawing as unobtrusively as possible with his knife, but it was impenetrable.

His mother said blandly with a faint kind of interest, "Is it all right?"

Avoiding her eyes, he pointed at his old man with his fork. "Why do you think I haven't been back for all these years?"

"Because you were scared it'd cost you something."

He picked up a piece of toast and aimed the edge of it between his old man's eyes, and he tried to think of the reason. He ought to be able to say it, put words around it, give it names, but they weren't coming. To fill up the stage-wait, he bit the toast, and his teeth didn't meet

181

through the middle of it. He took it carefully out of his mouth and looked at it and just as carefully said, "Mother, this toast is made out of plastic."

She said, "I'm not sure what they make it out of. I don't bake any more myself."

"Flour, water, and yeast, for Christ's sake," his old man said. "Any kid knows that."

He held it out. "I'm telling you it's a piece of plastic toast from a joke store or some place." He waited, but neither of them cracked a smile. "Aren't you going to laugh? I mean, you pull a joke, you might as well get a laugh out of it, even it it isn't funny."

"Something's wrong with your teeth, Hermie," his old man said. "If you've got plastic teeth, probably everything tastes like plastic."

His mother said, "I don't know how it happened. It must be all the commotion."

But she said it so mildly and calmly it made him mad. He said, "What commotion? You call this a commotion? You should've been in my hotel last night, you'd have heard a commotion."

"That's no way to talk to your mother," his old man said. "What?"

"Making indecent proposals. Keep your filthy hotels to yourself." His old man smiled like a pool player who'd just sunk a good one.

Raising his voice over the wind machine, he said, "I come home for a visit after a long—a long absence, and what do I get? A welcome? A kiss? A little music maybe?"

His old man said, "You want a kiss?"

"I get a piece of plastic toast and a—what?" He tried to

182

spear the steak with his fork so he could hold it up, but it wouldn't catch. "I get a glass of milk that tastes like it came out of a mechanical cow the hard way. Then I get accused of making a commotion."

"Not you," his mother said. "It's having your brother here."

"Talk to the guys on the rain machine, they're making the commotion." He paused, realizing he was doing a big take. "My what? What brother? I don't have a brother."

"It's a lot of extra work," his mother said. "But he's only staying for a month."

"Has to get back to college," his old man said.

Popsy sat still and tried to examine their faces in the poor light, but he couldn't see any sign of giggling or jiggling, no sign of them breaking up. "You're telling me I've got a brother?"

His mother went on, "So sometimes my cooking isn't as good as it used to be, it's the extra work."

He closed his eyes and tried to take one thing at a time. "How old is he supposed to be?"

His mother said, "Oh, about—what?"

"Nineteen, twenty," his old man said.

She said, "He's big for his age."

He squeezed his eyelids and pinched the bridge of his nose. The rain machine had settled down to a steady pummeling, like thousands of moths trying to get through the window screens at the same time.

Keeping calm, he said, "Twenty years ago, Mom, you were approximately fifty-five years old."

"That's right."

He waited, but apparently neither of them was going to

183

say anything else. They stood in the amber light looking pleased with themselves. His old man yawned noisily, not covering his mouth. Popsy said, "Who the hell's your dialogue coach? Who did this scene?"

"What's wrong?" his mother said.

"There's nothing wrong with adoption if you get the right size and color," his old man said.

"What did you want to go and adopt a kid for? You knew you weren't any good at raising kids. Wasn't I proof enough?"

Scratching himself and strolling toward the kitchen, his old man said, "You don't prove *any*thing, believe me." He glanced back at the table. "What about *my* dinner? I'm not eating that kind of crap."

Popsy shoved his chair out of the way and stood up. "You expect me to believe you?" The top of his head was almost level with the chandelier, and he had to squint against the light. "You'd have told me. You'd have said something."

"Why should we have to tell you anything?" his old man said.

"We were going to, but—"

"But what?"

His old man came back into the room abruptly and said, "That's all. No more noise."

"Who's making noise?"

"We reserve the right to refuse service to anyone, regardless of race, color, or creed."

Popsy took another look at both of them, but it didn't seem like a very good look: he couldn't read their expressions because they were dead-panning it so skillfully—like character actors who'd been told so often they had character in their faces, they'd quit trying to move.

His old man said, "Besides that, I want to break it to you gently, Herman, just in case you can't tell the difference any more—and I don't think it's exactly fair to your mother—your fly's open."

He checked quickly, and it wasn't, and he felt like a kid on a playground who'd just been caught by the oldest joke in town. Circling half the table, he got his old man in a blurry closeup, having to hunch his neck a little to stare straight into those gray eyes that had always looked cataracted. "You're telling me I really have a young brother?"

"Yes."

"A nice toy brother with a little handle on it that goes wee-wee and two changes of clothes? Does he light up in the dark, for godsake? What is this, a skit for Medicare?"

His mother said, "Well, he'll be down in a bit to get his dinner. You two can get to know each other, maybe, but no swearing."

He concentrated on his old man's eyes, but they didn't turn shifty or waver much. "All right, go call him."

"Sure." His old man went straight to the unlit stairway and started up.

"Wait a minute."

His old man stopped, and feeling panicky, Popsy said, "If you want off the hook, I'll tell you how to do it. When you get up there, plug in one of the auxiliary mikes, and if you want to make the sound of socking somebody in the jaw, slap your wrist with a wet powderpuff. Then open a window, loud—or if you really want to do it right and you don't happen to have a glass-crasher, kick the window out

185

and right away dump a bucket full of wet rags out on the sidewalk. Then come on back down and tell me he committed suicide and I can meet him some other time. Okay?"

Smiling and shaking his head in the shadows, his old man started up the stairs again, and Popsy edged back toward his mother in the kitchen doorway. The guys outside tried the rain and wind machines and the thunder screen all at the same time, but it wasn't very convincing. He said, "Look, I don't doubt there's somebody up there, but why don't you just say it's the boarder or the ice-man or somebody's long-lost nephew from Tacoma? I'd believe you then."

She said, "I can't help it."

During a sudden lull in the sound effects, he could hear two sets of feet crossing the ceiling, so unless his old man was doing something complicated with an extra pair of shoes and a couple of broomsticks, two people were going to come down the stairs.

And then they did, and he backed slightly toward the kitchen door just in case. But the young man coming down ahead of his old man had two legs and two arms and rusty-colored hair and a broad Slavic deadpan and slacks and a white shirt. He was two or three inches taller than Popsy and acted like somebody who'd been sent down from the slow-learners' class to the principal's office with a note and had forgotten why he'd come.

His old man said, "Richard, this here's your brother Herman."

The young man held out his hand, and Popsy reached over the back of a dining-room chair and shook it quickly without getting caught. It was a real hand, and he said, "At least you thought up a better name for *him*."

His mother said, "Did you make your bed?"

The young man nodded, then leaned forward and kissed her on the lips.

"Did you do your homework?" his old man said.

"Yes." The young man turned and kissed his father on the cheek.

Popsy watched him doing it, and it was like watching a geek eat a lightbulb in a sideshow. He managed to say, "What homework? It's still summer. He's not at school, he's home."

"Where the hell else you supposed to do homework?" his old man said. "And besides, what do you know about schools? You never stayed inside long enough to—"

"I'm—I'm getting an honorary degree from City College." He heard his old man go on making wise remarks, but he didn't feel like thinking up any comebacks. The young man was just standing there calmly, as if he wasn't listening either, his smooth flat face aimed at nobody. Yet it didn't seem like poise or good manners or good nature; it was machine-made, an atmosphere like something coming out of an air-conditioner. Popsy backed up another step, keeping out of arm's reach, and said, "Well, they're making them cordless now. Do you have to leave him plugged in all night?"

"No, the electric blankets don't work any more since I washed them," his mother said.

He kept his eyes on the young man, who was looking pleasant and ready to lend anybody a helping hand with the dishes or the garbage or the cases of empty beer bottles or mopping or a flat tire, and then it dawned on him, already a conviction before he'd even finished thinking it. He interrupted his old man in the middle of a sentence. "My God, look at him."

His mother said, "What?"

The young man's dark eyes turned on him then, finally, not exactly thinking but absorbing, and his old man said, "Now don't go starting anything."

Popsy said, "He's going to be a cop. Can't you see it? It's written all over him." The special-effects boys shook the thunder screen. "An honest cop."

"That's a lie," his old man said. "You can't make cracks like that about a kid of mine."

Something had gone definitely wrong with his stomach, and he had to save it, carry it out of here like a football with one arm around it, or he was going to lose it completely. He couldn't fumble it in his own end-zone because then even if he fell on it himself he'd lose points, and he couldn't afford to lose any more points.

His old man was still doing the talking, but Popsy turned away and headed toward his mother, who was blocking the doorway without trying to, her hips resting easily against both jambs.

He said, "I want out," and he tried to fake her out of the way without touching her, lowering one shoulder as if to give her an elbow in the stomach.

She backed around the corner into the kitchen, saying, "You two boys ought to be—"

He got into the storeroom without looking back and under the hinged bartop without being blocked by the bartender. The same row of behinds were perched on the stools, and while he peeled off twenties onto the service tray near the beer-taps, he raised his voice through the ruckus and said, "Okay, that's all for today. Principals and crew on nine o'clock call tomorrow morning, shooting outdoors if the weather's good. We won't need any of you guys at the bar any more, but stick around, we may need you in the big accident and explosion scene next week." He turned and swept his arm at the tables and the walls and the jukebox and the ads and the stinking air and all the rest of the junk. "And you can strike this set right now. We don't need it."

And on the way out he was glad to notice nobody gave him any backtalk. Instead, there was a respectful silence, which was more like it, and when he stepped out into the slow steady rain and headed for his truck, he checked the quality of the sound and it was pretty good, and whoever had been working the heavy weather had apparently knocked off for dinner.

Open your grab bag, Baby, let somebody try.
If it's empty, Baby, you can lie down and die.
But if anything's worth grabbing, you'll know the
reason why.

Chapter nine

The doorman said, "You can't leave it there much longer, Mr. Meadows. I'll get canned."

Popsy hoisted his two suitcases up over the side of the truck onto the flat-bed, then ducked back under the canopy out of the steady rain. "I paid you, didn't I? Now I need something to cover the bags."

Two black limousines were idling behind the truck, and one of them honked. Giving a *hold it* signal with one hand, the doorman said, "People don't like crawling out in the rain. Come on, now."

"Look, how about selling me your cape?" It was knee-length hard-woven black wool and didn't have the hotel's name stitched all over it.

Both limousines honked, and the doorman said, "Why don't you just throw your bags in the cab and forget it?"

"Forty? Sixty? Eighty?" Popsy peeled the money, waiting for the expression to change. "A hundred?" It changed, and he helped unhook the cape's high collar while the doorman motioned feebly at an elderly couple in evening dress climbing out of the second limousine before their chauffeur could get around to the curbside door.

The woman came dripping under the canopy first, holding a jeweled purse over her head. She took a look at Popsy and pinched her mouth down on one side. "I might have known."

He got the cape loose and tried it on, then got the stack of records off the sidewalk and onto the co-pilot's seat, balancing them on the bottles. Leaving the door open, he ducked under the canopy again and tried to remember whether he'd forgotten anything. But it felt more like trying to forget whether he'd remembered anything. The late evening traffic was swishing by on the wet pavement; headlights and taillights and stoplights and streetlights and neon signs were glancing off and rebounding from everything, even from places in midair where there was nothing except rain.

Then the doorman was back, sounding worried. "Maybe you better take your dough back, Mr. Meadows. What the hell am I going to tell the manager?"

But he didn't have time to start an advice column now because Stutz was coming out of the hotel door, all suntanned and wearing an orange cocktail dress that went out into some kind of screwy flounces three inches above her knees, and she'd lost at least ten pounds since he'd seen her last.

She said, "You told me you were going to turn on the shower, but this is ridiculous. Turn it off, Popsy."

He felt embarrassed. "Hi."

191

"I couldn't find you in Chicago, so I figured you must be some place else. Pretty shrewd, huh?"

"Yeah." He shook the cape and wiped the rain off his forehead, not looking her in the eye.

She said, "I found a couple of what you might call clues in the paper, and since I'd already come all the way from good old Miami by hand, I said to myself, 'What's a couple of hundred more miles between friends?' and so here I am, you worthless sonofabitch."

"Don't get mad, Stutz. I thought you'd know it was a gag."

"I knew it was very very funny, but I didn't know it was a gag."

"At least I was right about one thing: I told you you looked great, and look at you." She was shivering a little, so he put the cape over her shoulders. Then he noticed she was staring at the truck. "I'm checking out."

"I know you're checking out. They told me at the desk you were checking out. So go ahead and check out and good luck, and don't drop dead right away. Wait till I get out of town, so nobody'll blame me."

The doorman said, "Mr. Meadows, if you don't move that heap, I'll have to call a cop."

"So where's the party?" Stutz said.

"We had one but it died."

The doorman said, "I'm telling you, Mr. Meadows."

Two taxis were behind the limousines now, starting to honk, and Popsy said, "Come on, let's have a drink." He held the door for her, gave her a boost up when she hesitated, then helped scrape the records and bottles onto the floor so she could sit down. "It ain't much but it's home."

192

When he came around to the driver's side and hunched in out of the rain, she said, "You mean have a drink in here? Have you gone native?"

He got it started and pulled out into the traffic. "No. I know a place. What time is it?"

"Nine forty-five. Why don't we just check back in? I'm mad at you, but I'm not *that* mad." She shifted her feet among the junk. "I don't have any toes in my shoes. And I don't see you in two years—or three?—and you don't even kiss me."

"I'll kiss you."

"Soon as we get safely in public, right? Just to give my husband a thrill. I don't know what gets into me sometimes —Chicago was bad enough, but *here*."

All the lights coming through the dripping windshield seemed to turn red at once, so he took the hint and stopped. Without hitting anything. "It's not bad, but if you don't like it, maybe we'll go somewhere else. Enjoy yourself."

"I'm not exactly the old gray mare, you know."

"That's what I meant. I—"

"I may be pushing forty, but at least I—"

"If you're tired of pushing, pull for a while." Most of the red lights started moving again, so he kept up with them.

She said, "But at least I'm happily married, which is more than you can say."

"Must've been a long wait in the cocktail lounge. Nobody to talk to except the bartender and those nice friendly salesmen."

"What do you know about it?" She sounded mad.

"I'm psychic."

"They were engineers, agricultural engineers, and if we

had a few more people making an honest living like that—"

"They'd put Miami back under water." He turned into what seemed to be the right street, slowed down while he squinted past the wipers at the neon signs ahead, and found the one saying THE FINGER.

"What was I supposed to do, sit in the lobby and wait? I want some spending money including plane fare unless you've cheapened up in your old age. And I'd like it now, please, not when we're finished."

"Finished what?" The street was solid with parked cars, so he wedged the truck at an angle into the nearest half space, turned off the ignition, and got out his checkbook.

"If I'm going to force myself to be cheery and bright, I want something out of it. What you give best is checks. I wouldn't count on anything else."

He braced the book on the steering wheel and started scrawling. "I married you once, didn't I?"

"Don't remind me." She took the check and bent forward into the faint light, examining it, then said sarcastically, "Sure you can spare it?"

He got out into the rain. "Prices gone up?" He slammed the door on her reply, but went around and helped her out the other side.

After scrambling into a doorway till she could get the cape adjusted, she looked him over carefully. "What's the matter with you? You don't act like yourself unless maybe you've got a date to get lynched tomorrow."

He let her look, even let her see under his eyelids if the light was good enough, opened up the front of his face and gave her a peek. He said, "I'm alone. But don't tell anybody."

194

She peered up at him, tilting her head. "Are you trying to tell me something?"

"The truth, but don't let it bother you. Come on, when I count three, we go." He got her firmly by the hand.

"I'm in heels."

He counted, then dragged her in a wobbly sprint toward the entrance, and by the time they were panting between the cashier's desk and the hatcheck stand, his blood was going again.

Stutz said, "You call this being alone?"

The Finger was almost as jammed as the last time he'd seen it, but the people were mostly sitting down instead of standing up, and there were no portable TV cameras in the aisle. He wedged himself past the wall that screened the first of the long row of booths and started looking for Belle in case she'd decided to be on time to teach him a lesson. But the fog was too thick in the room already to see much except what was on stage where the lights were aiming.

The singing kid and the girl, Rachel, had apparently just done something worth doing because they were getting a big hand for it and, under the kid's lead, weren't even killing the applause by milking it too long. Maybe they'd never even left the stage once he'd gotten them started. But then he noticed the kid was wearing a tux with a frilly dress shirt, and the girl had on some kind of white satin minidress with a white veil snarled somehow or other through her long blond hair like a piece of toilet paper caught in a bush. She was also carrying what looked a whole lot like a wedding bouquet, all of which wasn't a bad idea for a novelty, but they'd have to close their act with it or else get off for some kind of complicated costume change—a very bad idea in a small club with a small stage —and he was in the middle of lining out a routine for them, a list of songs they could use without having to crawl in and out of the combo to the stage door in order to get more props, when Stutz rammed him in the ribs and said, "Don't you even have a table reserved?"

The nearest people were beginning to recognize him, and for a moment he considered ducking around to the alley entrance, but then the kid and the girl started singing a rock version of "Because" which seemed to bother several older customers at the bar and in booths: they hollered in protest.

Stutz said, "Let's get out of here."

But he held onto her, enjoying the hassle over the National Anthem of Newlyweds and wishing Richie were along to back them up with the dirty version. One woman was dragging her husband out of a nearby booth like a laundry bag, and before anybody else could slide in, Popsy hauled Stutz into the opposite side and took their places. The kid and the girl were picking up alternate phrases now, handing the number back and forth as if they'd been rehearsing for six weeks, and the kid had had some of the raucous quality knocked out of his voice by getting hit in the nose.

To Stutz he said, "How do you like the kid? A pupil of mine."

"He's cute."

"I mean his voice." He had to practically nuzzle her ear to make himself heard.

"Sounds like you on a bad day."

"Then he must sound like me all the time."

In the middle of a phrase the kid saw him and went right up in the words, mouth open, nothing coming out, and the girl apparently thought it was a gag because she started doing it too, and they finished the whole last chunk in pantomime with their hands outstretched toward Popsy. Someone swiveled one of the baby spots at the edge of the stage till it was right in his eyes, and that was the end of that.

Stutz said, "Oh, for Christ's sake."

The combo was rattling and rumbling to a finish and people were clapping and he muttered to Stutz, "Take it easy," but didn't know whether she could hear him. She tried to slide out but he held her.

And when you were in the spotlight there was really only one thing to do and that was stay in it till you did something worth looking at or listening to, something that gave you the right to get back into the dark. The only trouble was he couldn't think of anything worth looking at or listening to, so meanwhile he smiled.

The kid said, "And we owe it all to Popsy."

Waving his free hand at the applause, Popsy kept quiet and kept Stutz quiet by squeezing her wrist below the edge of the table.

From the stage the girl used the standing mike to say, "This one's for you, big man."

The two of them joined hands, backed away from the mike while the combo went zooming down into a slow heavy rock beat like a machine throwing wreckage into some huge metal container one scoop at a time. The name painted on the bass drum was The Earaches, and Popsy felt like a believer. When the spotlight switched back to the stage, he flattened his free hand against one ear.

Stutz said, "Oh, God, let's get out of here. My husband—"

The girl sang:

> I'm gonna marry you
> No matter what you do.
> I'm gonna live with you
> No matter who you are tomorrow ...

People were gathering in front of the booth in the semidark to get a better look, and though it wasn't as big a crush as the night before, soon there was a solid lineup and he had to go into a half crouch to see the stage.

The kid sang:

> If you say I do,
> Well, I will too.
> We'll split the difference
> Into joy and sorrow ...

The voice still had an edge to it like an old razorblade, in spite of the improvement, and sooner or later the kid would have to let the sound come from somewhere lower than his wishbone.

One of the silhouettes between him and the stage said, "I'd like to introduce myself."

"Go away," Stutz said.

She sounded mean, and he tightened his hold on her wrist to keep her from starting anything.

The girl pointed through the smoky beam of the spotlight at him and sang:

> I've been
> Getting in
> On the wrong side of bed too long.

Please, please,
Move me
Over to the right side from now on.

The silhouette said, "We were in high school together, and I—"

Stutz said, "We're trying to listen."

"Don't you remember the time we—" and the voice went on. It was probably either male or female, but he couldn't tell which.

"I remember everything," Popsy said. "I love you dearly, but please go away."

Through it the kid and girl sang together:

King size
Or queen size,
We'll be the sleep in each other's eyes . . .

The magnum of champagne stuck out of its oversized bucket like a replica of some giant cannon laying siege to the booth, and for the fifth or sixth time the kid wrestled it out, cradled it in both forearms, and filled their glasses, jabbering away and spilling more than usual.

Stutz had calmed down and was trying to act charming, and the girl was being mostly quiet, and Popsy felt he needed to blink his mind. There was something in it, something in the corner of it that wouldn't come out, a loose lash or a cinder of a thought scratching him. Automatically he got out his handkerchief and touched his forehead with it, then both his real eyes, but there was no way to reach his mind's eye and fix it.

Stutz said, "I thought it was only mothers that bawled at weddings."

When he took the handkerchief away, she was looking at him. He said, "Smoke. But I'm old enough to be their mother. You want to be their old man?"

"We'd never-a thought of it if you hadn't got us on stage," the kid said. "And we want you to be best man."

Popsy said, "Thanks. I'm touched."

"Besides, it'd be better publicity," the kid said, maneuvering the magnum back into its bucket.

Now the neck and its open hole were aimed directly at Popsy, and he shied a little sideways, bumping the girl.

She said, "Did we really sound okay? We needed a lot more rehearsing, and I don't think that 'Because' thing even gets halfway out of the bag. I think we ought to—"

Popsy said, "I'll tell you what I think. If you give a little more room to build—"

A middle-aged woman in a corset and a black dress squeezed past the bucket-stand, leaned over the table, and handed him a menu. "Could I have your autograph, Mr. Meadows? I'm one of your oldest fans. I mean longest." Her chuckling melted into the crowd noise.

He signed it next to the roast beef, gave it back without looking, and said to the girl, "The trouble is the song just seems funny at first, but if you give people time to start listening, then you can get tough with them."

The woman had stayed put, looking annoyed. "Is *that* your signature?"

"What is this, a bank?" The kid began tickling the woman at the waist. "Lady, this is a private party here, and—"

Looking from the menu to Popsy and squinting in the gloom, the woman said, "Even if it's a joke, I think President Kennedy's family ought to be told about it." She

200

squirmed out of the kid's reach. "There's probably a law."

Stutz polished off her champagne and turned the glass upside down on the table. "It doesn't tickle my nose any more, but it sure has learned its way around the rest of me."

"Go on, Mr. Meadows," the girl said. "I really value your advice."

"Yeah," the kid said.

"Well, your voices grate together a little, not badly, but it'll get worse unless you get somebody to hit Serge in the beak every couple days. And singing in unison gets boring. One of you'll have to sing harmony or scat or counterpoint or something." The girl had her hand on the cushion beside his leg which was a little distracting, and when she started to move it, he held on.

Stutz said something and the kid said something and the girl said, "He can't sing harmony, I've heard him try. He goes flat."

"Who says I go flat?" The kid finished what was left in the stem of his glass and reached for the magnum.

Popsy said, "The last time I was a best man was when Richie tried to marry a waitress without a license and wound up in a fistfight with a priest. So don't forget the license."

"All we have to do is drive to the other side of the river," the girl said. "They've changed the laws over there."

Under the table he put her hand carefully into her lap and left his own with it for a moment.

Looking bleary-eyed and a little loose in the jaw, the kid said, "Popsy, you ought to get married. You haven't been married lately. They've got justice-of-the-peaces over the river."

Stutz said, "Being married's like being an Arab with a

camel's hair coat—you know it's supposed to be good, but it reminds you of something that stinks."

A couple more people had come up to the table's edge and were leaning into the booth to listen, and the kid got up and elbowed the nearest man. "If you're going to table-hop, keep hopping."

The man said, "I'm Jim Eddy of *Time*. Celebrating something?"

When Popsy tried to slide out of the booth, the girl stayed put and showed his hand what to do, which he already happened to know by heart in all keys, major and minor, but he kept sliding toward her on the seat and finally forced her out into the aisle. While he struggled to his feet, he said, "I'll be right back," and then to the others, "I'll be right back, don't go away, and keep some bubbly on the back of the stove because I'm hungry. Nature calls."

They said various things which he didn't exactly memorize, and then he was squeezing through the Great Unwashed again, the gang that was always the same people even in his nonexistent hometown which must have had to hire them especially for the weekend and fly them in from one of the coasts: the lapel massagers, the pinchers, the ones who had a wonderful idea for a gag that was going cheap, the songwriters who didn't know much about music but who could hum it for him, the outright feelers, male and female, the weight guessers, the remember-whenners, guys up on booze or pot who could imitate his next-to-last record word for word except the high notes and low notes, the ones who had always loved him no matter what their friends said, dames who wanted to smear lipstick on him somewhere, anywhere, just to be able to say they didn't

202

feel anything special afterward, the moochers and the smoochers and the mutual friends and the pari-mutuel friends, and by the time he broke into a comparatively clear space near the rear end of the bar, he wasn't sure whether he'd been able to see into all the booths or not, and he wasn't even sure he could remember what Belle looked like.

He took a good squint into the last booth and the next-to-last booth, but they seemed to be full of cut-out black-and-white underexposed enlargements of people from some old nightclub publicity shots, and she was at least in natural colors, he could remember that, and three dimensions.

Somebody behind him had hold of his elbow and was telling him the middle of a joke, and he turned around and said, "What time is it?"

"Eleven-thirty. Jesus, it's great being able to talk to you. Now I want you to get this build-up to the—"

Three dimensions and brown hair sort of wavy, he remembered, and about five feet five. There were a lot of other details that would come to him if he had a little peace and quiet to think about them, and of course if he could actually see her, then he wouldn't have to try to remember.

People in the nearest booth were shouting requests at him now, three or four different numbers, and arguing a little between shouts. Belle wasn't at the bar either, as far as he could tell from the rear views of rears, and it dawned on him that she wasn't anywhere now, that he wasn't going to see her, that she didn't want any part of him, especially not the parts that counted, and that therefore he wasn't going to have to haul up his memory like some old lunker catfish out of a mudhole to recall her looks and likes

203

and dislikes and hotlicks, because it was all off and he could haul off and start over again somewhere else, from scratch not from the Valley of the Shadow of the Eightball. They were through, and now he could fall in love again without having to *be* in it. Or maybe he'd just skip it altogether, if possible. And the minute he thought it, he knew it wasn't possible.

A sinewy woman wearing a hard brassière had got hold of the opposite arm from the joker and was rubbing herself against his thigh, saying, "Sing, Popsy, go on, sing." And it seemed to be a pretty popular idea because more than half a dozen people stopped saying whatever else they'd been saying and started using phrases with *sing* in them. And these gradually coalesced into "Sing, Popsy, sing, Popsy, sing, Popsy" until the whole back half of the club was chanting at him.

He gave a last look along the middle booths, having to keep his elbows up against people who were milling around or waving at him up close as though he couldn't see their hands in front of his face or leaning in toward his ears to tell him to sing. He said, "Entertain yourselves, all you lovely people. Think up something yourselves, for godsake."

If anybody heard him, it didn't show. One man had a hand on his shoulder, waggling him, and was saying, "Who? Who? Who? Who? Who?" over and over, and either it was a request or the guy was an owl, but he kept it up till Popsy got hold of his necktie and pulled him close enough to holler, "Sing it yourself!"

That quieted a few people nearby, and a couple of boothfuls stood up, thinking maybe it was the start of a fight, but it wasn't. He let the guy go and held out his arms like wings and flapped them a little. He didn't take off, but even more people shut up; and while he waited for a moment one of his arms got caught in the crowd in front of the barstools and somebody started trying to work the ruby off his ring finger. Pulling in his arms, he said, "I've got an announcement."

Several jokers began shouting "Quiet" like assistant directors, and after that, things settled down pretty much. He glanced around the whole smoky jam-up, his home away from home, Ulcerville where the elite meet to compete, Lush College, the land of the naked tonsil, with an empty stage behind him and a mike waiting for somebody to make its electronic gizzard vibrate, and he said, "I'd like to announce—" again he waited for some more simmering down "—I'd like to announce my forthcoming marriage to somebody. Thank you, and all my love to one and all." He gave a bow and a dismissing smile, neither of which probably did much good in the near-dark, then started back to the booth.

The grabbers and wheedlers and friskers and storytellers were as thick as ever, but he brushed them off and managed to catch a waiter. Holding on to the opposite side of the waiter's full tray, Popsy said, "Look, I want two magnums of champagne to go. How much?"

"How about some small bottles, Mr. Meadows?"

"No, they're too easy to lose track of. Two magnums. How much?"

The kid was doing a pretty good job of driving the truck, considering how hard it was to pass the magnums

205

around and get swigs out of them without hitting somebody or cracking them together or banging the windshield.
The rain had slowed to a drizzle, which didn't matter from
where Popsy was sitting: under the girl wedged sideways
against the passenger's door with Stutz in the middle of the
seat, helping work the steering wheel.

They got off the bridge all right and went skidding
around a cloverleaf into the next state where the bars were
still open and the smear of neon along the ramshackle
waterfront stretched as far as he could see. When he
squinted past the girl's shoulder, it all turned into do-it-
yourself rainbows.

The girl started giving the kid directions, sounding too
sober, so when Stutz slid one magnum over toward him
he took an extra dose or two to loosen her up a little in his
own ears at least. She took a little ritual sip of it herself,
having to flap her long hair out of the way and tilt her
head sideways near the ceiling while he supported the cold
bottom. Her own bottom was planted so firmly in his lap,
he wasn't sure what the state of affairs was going to be
when they got out of the truck. Maybe they wouldn't
come apart, and the best man would have to come down
the aisle with her like a fireman. Or maybe there wouldn't
be an aisle.

He said, "Do justice-of-the-peaces have aisles?"

Stutz said, "Get some sleep. Don't worry."

"Who's worried? What have I got to worry about?" But
he immediately started to worry. He felt his brow crinkle
and the sweat start at his temples, but he didn't know
what he was worrying about.

"I'm already married," Stutz said. "So there's nothing to
be afraid of."

206

He'd watched so many women come down aisles. It was like watching them come late to a Broadway show, hanging on to their daddies' arms or their low-calorie artificially sweetened daddies, and one had left him for a prince and one had left him for a horse and a couple had never let go of their daddies' arms at all, and Stutz had left him to get a little rest, and there'd been the dozens who hadn't quite made it to the aisles or the church or the right town, not counting the just plain engagements, up like a rocket and down like a stick. Maybe it was all part of growing up.

He said, "You're never too old to grow up."

The girl kissed him for the first time, breaking the ice and almost breaking a front tooth when the kid turned right into a rutted driveway, and he gave her a good one back, one of his specials with a minimum of champagne in it, and they were still getting the good of it when the truck stopped and the kid said, "Hey, leave some of that for me."

Popsy pulled back for a moment to give him a reasonable explanation, since all members of the younger generation were entitled to reasonable explanations of natural phenomena and not fairy stories, but the kid had been talking about the nearest magnum, and while he and Stutz juggled it back and forth, Popsy went back to the girl who seemed to be trying to tell him something without words, which in the long run was the best way to get your message across to slow learners. He got a good taste of her message and felt it to make sure it was real.

Stutz said, "I hate to butt in, but—"

The kid interrupted her, getting both arms inside the doorman's cape, and the four of them necked for a few minutes.

Then the *Time* man opened the passenger's door and said, "Well, is it on or off?"

Keeping the girl from falling out backwards, Popsy said, "What do you care? You get paid by the hour, don't you?"

"Yeah, but it's wet out here."

Stutz said, "Well, you can't come inside 'cause there's nothing extra to hang on to."

The kid opened the driver's door and got himself and both magnums out without spillage or breakage, and when Stutz followed him, there was enough room for Popsy to maneuver out from under the girl and then help her down to the ground floor. The photographer behind the *Time* man was taking pictures as fast as he could work his flashbulbs.

Then they were all in the driveway under a blue neon JUSTICE OF THE PEACE that was crackling in the light drizzle. The kid said, "I don't know about this."

"Don't worry," Stutz said. "It doesn't hurt till later."

"I mean, I don't want to rush into anything. Rachel?"

The girl said, "Hi."

Trying to sound fatherly, Popsy put his arm around the kid's shoulder and said, "Look, you're too young for this kind of thing. Why don't you and Stutz go have a good time some place, and I'll get married instead. I mean, once more won't bother me."

Stutz said, "Wait a minute, I make my own connections."

He nodded and waved a small apology at her, then shook the kid a little to start him ticking.

"But we were just working up an act together." The kid was looking more and more sober, narrowing his eyes against the gusts of wind.

"You have to learn to sing by yourself first," Popsy said. "You can't just sweep your voice under the rug."

The girl said, "What am I, the rug?"

"Oh." Popsy turned to her and focused. "What do you say? Want to get married?" He didn't like the tone of his voice, so he changed it before she could tell him she didn't like it either. "I didn't mean to get too far ahead of you. Want to try it? I'm solvent."

"I thought maybe you were." She had to turn into the wind to keep the hair out of her eyes. "But I don't know."

The reporter was taking notes on a folded wad of copy paper, and Popsy said, "Got anything better to do?"

"I guess not," she said.

"See, I don't want to jeopardize my career," the kid said. He was having to move his feet slightly in order to stay in one place. "We don't have to go and get married just to sing together. I mean, we don't have to sing in the bathtub."

Going up onto the porch under the neon sign, Stutz said, "If anybody needs a bridesmaid or a witness, okay, but hurry it up or I won't be able to tell what the hell I'm looking at." She cradled one of the magnums like a baby and bent sideways to take a swig from it.

The flashgun only went off once while they all trooped up the steps and gave the knocker and doorbell a workout, and Popsy put his arm around the girl to keep her from shaking. The wind couldn't exactly whistle up her minidress—there wasn't enough room—but her knees were bent slightly and she had pulled her shoulders in to keep warm. He said, "You know, you really can sing."

Her eyes—big, blue, sober, and sharp—turned into his, and she held still, listening.

"You're very very good, and you're going to be better. You can support me in my old age."

She smiled slowly and shyly. "Okay. But are you crazy?"

"Not yet." She was even younger than Belle, but he couldn't help that. He said, "As a wedding present, I'll help you cut your first record."

The kid said, "What about *my* first record?"

"Yours too, only you'll have to do it through a charcoal filter if you don't have her to cover those damn overtones."

And then the door opened, and he got a load of the justice of the peace and his squat wife in identical bathrobes, looking and acting as though they'd been carved out of a block of ice by the chef at the Waldorf as a centerpiece for a morticians' banquet.

And for a little while he lost track of current events—he could always catch up in *Time*—such as who had to sign what, and who had to stand where, and how many bills he had to peel off the wad for various purposes like the American Newspaper Guild's Fund for More Sober Obituaries and the Justice of the Peaces' Fund to Help Pick Up the Pieces and the Miami Civic Betterment League and the Greece-Israel Musical Exchange Program. His needle had slipped out of the groove and was dragging across the record, and by the time he got readjusted, the kid was singing an arrangement of "I Love You Truly" right out of Ripley's "Believe It or Not," including the wrong words which Stutz kept trying to correct. The flashgun from time to time turned everything blue and blank.

And then he was actually standing up in front of the

man with the Good Book again, with the girl's arm hooked in his, listening to the responsive reading and sticking in the replies more or less where they belonged and borrowing Stutz's wedding ring strictly for the duration of the ceremony because, as she explained, she liked to have one along whenever she tried to get into a strange hotel with a comparative stranger (a quick kiss for the kid who was making out pretty well as a best man, considering he wasn't at his best) and he watched the icy-blue jaw of Mr. Justice chomp up and down on the words and spit out the pieces, and the flashgun kept popping. And he was invited to kiss the bride, which he did, and then he invited everybody else to kiss the bride in order to share the wealth, to spread a good thing around.

The *Time* man asked him what he thought about marriage, and he gave it a decent description without four-letter words. And then somebody turned off the lights.

They only stayed off a moment, but when they came on again, he was driving the truck and the girl was on the seat beside him and the headlights were glancing off the long rows of parked cars in some kind of crowded neighborhood. He wasn't exactly feeling his best, but when he focused on the girl he felt reassured: she wasn't being wiped out with panic, she didn't have both hands on the door handle, ready to jump, so he must have been driving okay.

Catching his eye, she said nervously, "Are we really married?"

"That's the way *I* remember it." He didn't have the slightest idea where Stutz and the kid were, but they were probably better off in a taxi.

She said, "Is it much further?"

He looked through the windshield, and absolutely everything seemed much further, so he didn't know what to say. Then the neighborhood started looking familiar and he realized what he'd probably had in mind, if you could call it a mind. He turned left at the next stop sign, and he was on his old block, the chopping block, slowing down gradually and double-parking in front of the dark house.

The lights were all off in the bar too and all the way down the block except at the roofing plant where they kept them on for good luck and to keep from losing their last bundle of shingles in the night.

She said, "Do we really have to?"

"Well, it's probably the last chance you'll get." He climbed down to the wet pavement and went around to her door and helped her out, and by that time the *Time* man and the photographer had organized themselves and were out of their car and trailing along up the walk to the porch steps.

The *Time* man said, "How do you feel, Popsy?"

"I've got a headache."

"I mean sentimental? Old memories?"

Holding the girl's hand, he went up to the dark screendoor and tried to find the buzzer, but there didn't seem to be any. When he pulled at the doorhandle it was stuck, so he yanked it open, and simultaneously a brilliant overhead porchlight switched on like a sunlamp and a loud bell like a downtown burglar alarm went off under the eaves where he could see it hanging like a hornet's nest.

The girl ran all the way back to the truck, and the *Time* man and the photographer were halfway down the narrow walk before they stopped, but he stayed put. And after a

212

minute when he could see lights switching on here and there down the other side of the street, the door in front of him opened a crack.

Nothing come out of it, not even the muzzle of a shotgun or the muzzle of a German shepherd, and the bell was still clanging away, so he had to raise his voice. "I wanted you to meet one of my wives."

He couldn't hear any answer, and he couldn't even tell whether it was his mother or his old man on the other side of the dark crack—or maybe his brother walking in somebody's sleep. "That's her out in the truck if you want to take a peek through the curtains. I figured you ought to see one of them." The flashgun was going off, and the reporter was edging up the stairs as if building up his courage, and Popsy got out his checkbook.

There was too much light to see by, so he scrawled off his signature the way he would have signed a tab in a nightclub. He did three of them, leaving the other spaces blank, and inserted them through the upright crack. He could see fingers take the other ends, and he said, "I wanted to give you a wedding present. And if my brother doesn't turn out right, buy another one."

He backed off, giving a little curtain-call salute, and passed the *Time* man and photographer on the way to the truck, keeping up the salute and the big smile for all concerned. The bell was still so loud, he didn't even have to pretend not to hear the reporter but just climbed in and drove off.

The girl said, "I'm sorry, I got cold feet."

He helped pull the doorman's cape over her bare legs and knees, realizing how decent that had been of Stutz on a cool night, and he said, "Mrs. Meadows, I'll take care of you."

"Thanks. Thanks, Popsy."

She was looking shy and afraid, and he tried to think of something to warm her up.

She said, "How far's the hotel?"

"Not very far." The *Time* man's headlights were shining in the rear-view mirror, and he took a deep breath and another deep breath and then swallowed at the lump in his throat. He said, "Why don't we sing something?" The lump felt like his voice box making some kind of limited return engagement. Something had made him weirdly happy.

She said, "Okay, but don't expect too much."

He said, "I won't." But he did, he always did. He held her hand, and when she opened her mouth, he opened his.